'WARE DANGER

'Ware Danger

A Patrick Dawlish Mystery

**John Creasey *writing as*
Gordon Ashe**

ISBN: 978-1-5040-9866-3

This edition published in 2025 by Open Road Integrated Media, Inc.
180 Maiden Lane
New York, NY 10038
www.openroadmedia.com

'WARE DANGER

CHAPTER ONE

DAWLISH IS RELUCTANT

Captain Patrick Dawlish sat in the corner of a first-class carriage, with his feet up on a newspaper-covered seat opposite him. The window by his side was misted over, the dim lamp above doing nothing to help what little daylight there was. His rugged face, which would have been handsome but for a broken nose, was set in a scowl which indicated that all was not right with his world.

He was a puzzled man.

Six hours before he had been prepared for yet another day of monotony at the north country camp where the 3rd East Loamshires appeared to have been stuck for duration.

To his frequent requests to serve overseas, his Commanding Officer had invariably given the same answer:

'You're very valuable here, Dawlish, you know. I'll do what I can for you, but I can't promise anything. Be patient for a bit, there's a good fellow.'

Days grew into weeks, weeks into months, Dawlish stayed where he was, until at half-past seven that morning he had been called to the C.O.'s billet, to find that friendly and amiable gentleman in the middle of shaving.

'Oh, Dawlish, good morning. I—er—I've instructions for you. Can you catch the eight-thirty from Doncaster?'

Dawlish's heart had leapt.

'For where, sir?'

'London, my boy, where else?'

'Is this a change at last?' Dawlish had asked. The C.O. shook his head.

'I don't think you're going out of the country, Dawlish, you're very valuable here, you know. In fact I've told them that I can't really spare you, but they've promised that you'll be back in a week or ten days. You'll report to Room 13 at the Clarion Hotel as soon as you get to Town. Don't ask me any more than that, I can't tell you. Good luck, my boy.' Benignly the C.O. had waved his razor in dismissal, and Dawlish had eaten a hurried breakfast and reached Doncaster in time for the 8.30 train. He had been too rushed to ponder much about the mysterious nature of his orders, but since he had settled down in his corner seat he had endeavoured to probe it. So far he had been unsuccessful. In fact he found himself more perturbed by the Colonel's 'I can't really spare you' than by his instructions; the old devil did not propose to let him go.

His gloomy thoughts were interrupted by a steward.

'First luncheon ready, sir.'

'Oh, thanks,' said Dawlish. 'Keep me a seat, will you?'

'Yessir, thank you, sir.' The man gave him a ticket and then went on to the next compartment, repeating his formula. He had not closed the door properly, and consequently his voice came clearly to Dawlish's ears; that did not matter, but the deep voice of the man who answered mattered a lot.

'Keep me a seat, steward. Can you send me a drink along first?'

'Sorry, sir, the staff's got to do the lunches. Serve you at the dining-car, sir, thank you, sir.'

The next compartment door slid to, but Dawlish was already in the corridor. For a moment he doubted the evidence of his own ears. The voice was surely unmistakable, but there seemed no reason why Ted Beresford should be on the train. Ted was supposed to be in Scotland, with the 5th Midshires. Ted's last letter had assured him of this.

It was Beresford.

Impossible to mistake him, there he sat in a compartment to himself, his largeness and solidity redeemed by a pair of merry grey eyes and a mobile, humorous mouth.

Dawlish peered at him through the sliding-door. Beresford's face was set in a scowl, but Dawlish himself was no longer dissatisfied; the world was a brighter, happier place. Led by the chink of crockery he arrived at the kitchen-cumbar and by producing a ten-shilling note he obtained two bottles of beer, glasses, and a tray. With these in hand he staggered back to Beresford's compartment and kicked open the door.

Beresford started up.

'Good Gad! I—no, it isn't! You can't be! Pat, you old devil, what *are* you doing here?' Tenderly he rescued the tray. 'How long have you been on the train?'

'Since Doncaster.'

'Doncaster!' moaned Beresford. 'I joined it there. And to think that I've been sitting alone in this benighted carriage parched with thirst!'

Dawlish extracted a bottle-opener from his pocket; he did not travel unprepared for good fortune. Solemnly he filled the glasses.

'To Joan, bless her.'

'Felicity, bless her,' said Beresford, and their compliments to each other's romances duly paid, they drank deeply. Beresford took out a cigarette-case, and as they lighted up he said more normally: 'How long have you got?'

'I'm not on leave,' said Dawlish. 'At least, I don't think I am. How long have you got?'

Beresford stared. 'I'm not on leave either,' he said.

'What?'

'It's a fact. At least I don't think I'm on leave.' He eyed lingeringly the inch of beer in his glass. 'The C.O. sent for me late last night—'

'Early this morning for me,' said Dawlish, and both men, although their smiles remained, had grown more tense.

'But they promised I wouldn't be more than a fortnight.'

'A week or ten days,' said Dawlish, and both men stared at each other oddly. Very deliberately, Beresford finished his beer.

'And could I catch the 1.30 from Edinburgh.'

'Eight-thirty, Doncaster.'

'For London, and report at—'

'Room 13,' said Dawlish after a pregnant pause.

'It must be,' said Beresford. 'It can't be anything else. The Clarion Hotel, as soon as I reach Town.'

'The same,' said Dawlish. He sat back in his corner and stared at his friend. 'It can't be coincidence,' he said. 'They wouldn't pick by accident on you and on me of all the tom-thumbs in England. Ted, it's a queer business before it starts. We're wanted, and we're wanted together. Have you the remotest idea what it's about?'

'I haven't an inkling,' said Beresford heavily. 'Except—I mean unless it's one of the old games.' His mouth broadened into a delighted grin. 'Pat, we're going to be under special orders, together! Something's up. By George, something's so far up that a Great White Chief thought of you, and that reminded him of me. Pat, we're on a spree! Don't look so gloomy, old chap, don't you like the sound of it?'

'I don't quite know,' said Dawlish slowly. 'After all, I spent six months begging for a commission, and I wanted it in the Army,

not Scotland Yard, and if it's what you think, the Yard's behind
it.' He shrugged. 'Oh, well, we'll know more about it in Room 13,
bless their little hearts. Let's go and feed.'

They left the compartment together, Beresford bringing up
the rear, and as he swayed from side to side he reflected on the
past, and the divers occasions when Pat Dawlish had worked
with Scotland Yard. He knew that beneath Dawlish's somewhat
heavy expression, there was a mind as keen as any in England.

They had good reason for remembering those things which
Dawlish humorously called 'incidents'. In the first one Beresford
had met Joan, in the fourth Dawlish had met Felicity. With them
had worked others—Bill Furningham and Timothy Jeremy,
among them. Before starting on these peculiar jobs Dawlish
had always been reluctant; he was not, he claimed, a policeman,
and he hoped that he would never become one. Yet once in the
midst of violence and the need for matching his wits against
those who had puzzled and often outwitted the police he had
acted as if it was his chosen vocation.

The dining-car was nearly empty.

Only seven other people were there, as far as Dawlish could
see; one was a woman modishly-dressed and more than good to
look upon. Her violet eyes stared as if unseeingly, but it passed
through Dawlish's mind that she might be fishing for company.
He was in no mood for small-talk with a stranger, and in any
case, his liking for casual acquaintances had dimmed considerably since he had known Felicity. He passed the woman, and
then he pulled up, staring at the single occupant of the table for
four by which he was standing. There was a short silence, and
then his voice and the single occupant's spoke together.

'Pat!'

'Timothy!'

'By all that's holy,' said Ted Beresford in a low voice—so low that only Dawlish and the woman could hear him, and he had forgotten the woman—'it can't be Room 13?'

Patrick Dawlish's voice, loud, boisterous, overlaid the last words. 'What stupendous luck! All on leave together, all on the same train, all going to drink and laze and talk the nights through—could it be better? I ask you, *could* it be better?'

He slid into a seat opposite Timothy, pumping his hand across the table.

As he did so the woman in the seat backing on his was marking the tablecloth with her fork. The impression on the cloth read:

'Room 13.'

CHAPTER TWO

THE LADY LINGERS

They ate heartily, drank not excessively, and talked with abandon, although not of Room 13. None who listened or overheard would have suspected that the three officers were not on leave, blessing the coincidence which not only gave them leave together, but also put them on the same train. They sobered somewhat when they discussed London.

'I've been up once since the bombing started,' said Timothy. 'It's put an end pretty effectively to fun and games by night, Pat.'

'You should know better than to want fun and games by night,' said Dawlish reprovingly. 'Ted and I don't.'

'I am not tied to any girl's apron strings,' said Timothy with relish. 'How you two stand it I don't know. And if either Joan or Felicity knew some of the interludes in your young lives they might not be as warmly disposed as they are.'

'One of these days you will fall,' said Ted hopefully.

'Heavily,' said Pat Dawlish.

'Not on your life,' said Timothy with confidence. 'I'm woman-proof.'

'Famous last words,' jeered Dawlish. 'My bet is that a pair of pretty eyes will lead you astray within five minutes of reaching Town. Do you remember that little red-head—Judy, wasn't she called?' he demanded of Beresford.

'And that Spanish lovely,' said Beresford with high relish. 'You know, the one who danced—'

'Be careful,' said Dawlish, 'this is a public dining-car.'

'A fandango on his dining-room table,' concluded Beresford solemnly. 'And there was the Irish colleen with the blue eyes, he followed her about like a dog for a fortnight.'

'I resent all these implications,' said Timothy Jeremy with feeling. 'I may amuse myself. I do not fall. What about moving?' he added. 'We've been here an hour as it is.'

Dawlish called for the bill. As they left the dining-car he saw the woman with the violet eyes. There was no doubt about it; she was looking at him, and meant him to see that she was looking. Meeting the steward further along the corridor Dawlish tapped him on the shoulder.

'Steward, do you remember the lady who was sitting next to us?'

The steward permitted himself a slight smile.

'Oh, yes, sir.'

'What part of the train is she on?'

'In the first-class carriages at the back, sir.'

'Good man,' said Dawlish. 'When she leaves the dining-car, slip along and tell me, will you?'

'Very glad to sir, thank you, sir.' The steward smiled again, and the trio went into Dawlish's compartment. He did not immediately sit down, but stood staring for some seconds at the window. Timothy took one corner as Ted closed the door.

'Now,' he said, 'perhaps you won't mind if we mention Room 13, Mr. Dawlish. There is such a thing as being over-cautious. False wigs and beards and all that. Who the blazes do you think is going to be interested in what room we're going to?'

'I've no idea,' said Dawlish mildly, 'but I hope to soon. Tim, haul your lazy self up and slip along to your compartment, will you? You too, Ted.' He turned and faced them, and there was a smile on his lips but not in his eyes. They had seen a similar expression often before, and they knew that Dawlish had seen something which puzzled him. They did not argue, and while Timothy Jeremy was in his compartment, Dawlish joined him.

'Well, what's it all about?' demanded Timothy. 'If it's a variation of musical chairs, I don't admire it, I—' he stopped as Dawlish stepped to the window, and indicated the mist on the inside. At one edge it was rubbed, as if someone had moved against it. 'What *are* you driving at, old man?'

'My dear Tim!' said Dawlish, 'use your eyes. This window's rubbed in exactly the same place that mine was. I'll lay odds that Ted's is the same.' He stood by the window and reached up to the luggage on the rack, and Timothy's eyes widened. 'Follow me?' asked Dawlish. 'Someone had a look at your luggage, and at mine—'

'We might have made the marks ourselves,' said Jeremy dubiously. 'Hang it, why should they look at our luggage?'

'Why should we be on the train?' demanded Dawlish. 'Did you reach up for anything before you left for lunch?'

'No-o.'

'Nor did I,' said Dawlish, 'and I'll bet the same mark is on Ted's window.' He went to Ted's compartment, to find Ted looking about him somewhat ruefully. As the others entered he said:

'I'm darned if I can see a thing, old man.'

'Poor old Ted,' said Timothy, looking at the window with an air of superiority. 'Can't you see that the window's been rubbed, that someone had stretched up to reach your luggage—or did you stretch up before you went to the luncheon-car?'

Ted Beresford stared.

'Eh? No. I didn't—it *has* been rubbed, by George! But I bet *you* didn't notice it.'

'And I thought I'd been convincing,' said Timothy Jeremy in mock despair. 'All right, Pat saw it. Odd business, isn't it?'

'Let's have a look at the stuff,' began Ted, but Dawlish stretched out an arm and stopped him.

'Later,' said Dawlish. 'People are passing up and down pretty frequently, and if a mysterious Mr. A did look at our luggage while we ate, the same gentleman might be wanting to know whether we've noticed it. We haven't, as far as he knows. Push the door right to, Ted, and close the window—we won't be over-heard if you'll keep that foghorn of yours tuned down.'

They settled themselves somewhat uncertainly.

'Well,' Dawlish said, 'what do we know? We get the same mysterious orders for the same possibly mysterious room, and our luggage, presumably, is searched. The orders could hardly have been so secret, could they?'

'Good Lord!' said Ted Beresford simply.

'What else?' demanded Tim.

'A sensible question,' applauded Dawlish. 'The other possibility is, of course, the lady who lingers.'

'If you mean that girl near us, you're daft,' said Ted.

'Maybe,' admitted Dawlish, 'but she was at the cheese-and-biscuits stage when we got there, and that suggests she was very hungry, or else she wanted to be in the dining-car before anyone else arrived. She couldn't have eaten cheese-and-biscuits for fifty minutes, which was the time we were there, yet she was still sitting when we came away. Lingering's the word.'

'She must be still at it,' said Tim drily. 'The steward is going to tell us when she's gone, isn't he?'

Dawlish shrugged. 'Unless I'm cock-eyed, you'll have further attention from her within the next three or four hours, Tim. We've registered a firm fact in her mind that Ted and I are one-woman men, and you're the profligate of the party. I—' he broke off, and looked round to find the steward opening the door.

'Beg pardon, sir, the lady went along to her carriage just after you. I couldn't get away before, sir, there was a rush.'

'That's all right, thanks,' smiled Dawlish, and he rewarded the steward suitably. When the door closed two pairs of eyes regarded him almost in awe.

'If she is interested in us,' said Ted profoundly, 'I'll withdraw all the rudery I've thought about you.' Both he and Jeremy gazed incredulously at Dawlish. They had known him for years yet never ceased to show astonishment at any indication of that peculiar sixth sense of his which appeared to work whenever there was the remotest suggestion of mystery. They could not get used to him. The rubbed windows, the possibility that their baggage had been searched, the forced conversation about Timothy's *affaires* and the calm and considered theorizing had come so swiftly upon each other that they had the appearance of being automatic; but the fact that the woman with the violet eyes had moved immediately after them, although she had lingered for so long, indicated one thing only; that she had wanted to hear what they said.

Timothy drew a deep breath.

'And so what?' he demanded.

'I think,' said Beresford, 'that I'd like to know who's in the compartment with her. Coast along the corridor, Tim, and make a point of looking into every first-class carriage. She won't be surprised now she knows what an amorous devil you are.' He chuckled as Timothy stood up with alacrity. 'There you are, you see—jumping at it.'

Tim gave a wide grin, then swayed along the corridor, for the train was travelling much faster. There were beams from a watery sun shining through fast-moving April clouds, and in the corridor the windows were now clear of mist. They were running through a small town, and Tim knew that in a little over an hour the journey to London would be over. He had no luck at the first section of first-class compartments, but at the next he saw the woman.

She was sitting in a corner, talking to a man opposite her. Tim saw her glance towards him as he looked through the glass panel, and he allowed his gaze to rest for a moment on her face; she was remarkably good to look upon. Her companion, a youngish man with jet black hair, glanced up at him also; no one else was in the carriage.

Timothy walked on to the end of the train, and then sauntered back. He drew near the woman's carriage while conscious of a slight increase in the beating of his heart. If Pat was right and she was interested in them, she might have made a move. If she appeared in the corridor and gave him an opportunity for forcing his acquaintance he would be prepared to admit that Dawlish *was* right.

He had to cross the steel plates between the carriages before he was able to see along her corridor, and consequently he knew nothing until he actually reached it. Then he saw her, standing by a window, looking out. As he came into sight she began to push it up with some difficulty. Jeremy went forward with an offer of help, hiding a grin at the thought that Dawlish had outwitted her.

CHAPTER THREE

AND THE LADY LURES

'I say,' said Jeremy, his sombre face relaxing into a smile which had considerable attraction, 'let me do that, please.' He reached the window, and began fiddling with it rather cunningly.

Violet eyes and auburn hair went well together, Tim decided; she was about thirty or so, he judged, although to an undiscerning eye she might have passed for much younger. Her make-up was carefully and not too freely applied; she was, in fact, a well-turned out woman of a type with whom Tim was familiar, and whose like—except that this one was better-looking—might in normal times be found in any Mayfair bar or party.

Her voice was attractive, too.

'How kind of you. I can never manage these windows.'

'I think the engineer who invented 'em was of a warped nature. You know the kind—no discomfort too much trouble.' He slid his cigarette-case out and offered it; she took one after a moment's hesitation, and he lit it for her.

'It wasn't a bad lunch, was it?'

'Did you—' she hesitated, and then laughed. 'No, I suppose it wasn't. I'm never sure whether it's more boring in the dining-car or in a compartment.'

Tim reflected that she had registered on him the fact that she was bored. 'Such a journey these days, too,' he said lightly. 'We're two hours late already, although I suppose we shouldn't grumble, things being as they are. Have you been to Town lately?'

'Oh, yes. I've been having a week with some friends in York. The quiet was heavenly.'

'And now back to the grind, eh?' said Tim. 'Too bad. As a matter of fact I wouldn't advise anyone who could get away to stay in London for long. Bad enough if you can't avoid it.' It was a fishing question, of course, and he wondered whether she would ignore it; he was relieved when she said:

'I'm trying to keep together the remnants of a business.'

'Oh, bad luck! The remnants, I mean.' Her eyes laughed at him; certainly thought Timothy, it would be easy to forget that Pat and Ted were further along the train, waiting for his report; he remembered a girl, what was her name? he had met in Paris three years before. She had similar violet eyes, and auburn hair. It had been a grand week or two, all clean and above board— Timothy was no philanderer for the sake of it, but he liked charming company.

'It is very nearly just that,' said the woman more soberly. 'Gowns and hats and fripperies.'

'I say!' exclaimed Timothy. 'What a game to keep that going these days! I suppose you've got one of those one-hat-only displays in the window. Intriguing, I always think—much more likely to lure the customer than half a dozen.'

'It's in Brake Street,' said his companion gently.

'Oh, of course. Ostentation definitely out. Odd thing. I have some friends living in a flat in Brake Street—over a jeweller's, Albertson's, do you know them?'

'They're at the other end,' she said.

She broke off as a man pushed past them. Timothy reflected that he was doing well, and that she was perhaps a little more informative than she should have been on so slight an acquaintance, if, indeed, it could be called one. On the other hand, the days of war had loosened tongues to strangers when, in pre-war days, a frozen silence would have been maintained.

'I wonder if—' he began.

An approaching guard demanded their tickets. He punched them, and went on. Timothy started again:

'I wonder if—'

'Excuse me,' said a large man who was coming towards them along the corridor, and they squeezed up and let him pass. Then they stared at each other, and with one accord they laughed.

'This is a bit hot, isn't it?' said Timothy. 'And half the train's empty. Look here, let's introduce ourselves. My name's Jeremy, Timothy Jeremy.'

She said simply: 'And mine is Julia Dawnay.'

'Dawnay,' said Timothy. 'Dawnay—I—by George, I've got it! My sister wanders in and out of the shop more or less as if she owns it.'

Julia Dawnay looked doubtful.

'Does she? I don't remember the name.'

'Oh, not Jeremy,' said Jeremy. 'Potter. She's one of the happily married. Don't say that you can't remember her,' he pleaded. 'She's positively lovely. We're supposed to be very much alike.' He presented so comical a countenance that she laughed again.

'Of course I know Mrs. Potter. I couldn't honestly say that I can see a likeness.'

'Too bad,' said Jeremy. His grey eyes twinkled at her. 'Look here, let's sit down. There isn't a crowd in your compartment is there?'

She hesitated.

'Just one, and I don't think he's said three words,' she admitted with a grimace. 'If we started to talk in there I think he'd protest.'

'Oh,' said Timothy. 'It's obvious to me that the man's not normal.' His smile was ingenuous, and she laughed again.

They walked desultorily along the corridor. None of the carriages there were empty, and as they reached the end of the carriage he grimaced.

'It's not our lucky day. Look here, my compartment's empty—it's at the end of the train.'

'But I thought you were with friends.'

Timothy chuckled.

'I'm glad you noticed the beggars. Not that you'd have much difficulty in noticing Pat Dawlish.' He stared at her as if with the birth of a new idea. 'I say, Miss Dawnay, why not come and join the crowd? They're quite human, if noisy, and'—he lowered his voice and went on confidentially—'between you and me, I shall have my leg most unmercifully pulled. If I don't show up soon, I mean.'

'I heard a little about your reputation,' said Julia Dawnay.

'Don't believe a word of it,' said Tim firmly. 'They're habitual liars where I'm concerned.' He gripped her arm to steady her as they went over the steel plates. 'I didn't know they were on the train until lunch-time. If we'd all got together earlier the journey wouldn't have seemed half as long.'

They reached the first-class carriage near the engine, to find Dawlish and Beresford with their legs stretched out, chattering as if they hadn't a care in the world. Both men jumped up when Tim slid the door back, and acknowledged his introductions gravely.

'Pity the journey's nearly over,' said Beresford.

'I'd just been saying so,' said Timothy. 'Cigarette, Miss

Dawnay?' She took one. 'What chance of getting some tea served in here?' he demanded, and pressed the bell for attendance. There was no difficulty, and they had tea. Dawlish did least of the talking, Ted and Tim competing for Julia Dawnay's attention with a keenness which, Dawlish thought, amused her as much as it did him.

He spent a little time assessing her.

He came to the same conclusion as Tim: she was a good-looking, admirably dressed and groomed woman of thirty or so, and she was nobody's fool. Her manner was completely unforced, and her low-pitched laughter was a good thing to hear. It passed through his mind that it was almost impossible to believe that she had deliberately angled for this meeting, and then he gave some thought to Tim and Ted. He was quite sure that no one in the world would suspect how neatly Tim had worked, and that they had all discussed the possibility of her interest not only in them but in the object of their trip to Town.

He wished a little ruefully that Ted had not mentioned Room 13, but wondered whether it really mattered.

The train was running into King's Cross before their tea-things were cleared away, and they had to break-up. There were several hours of daylight to go, and Timothy had insisted on seeing Julia Dawnay to her flat—which, she told them, was in Westminster.

'It's really too good of you,' said Julia. 'I shall be there in twenty minutes in a taxi.'

'Twenty minutes is a long time,' smiled Timothy. 'I can meet the others at the flat later.'

'"The" flat?' she said.

'We've joined forces,' explained Dawlish lightly. 'Timothy had a long lease, and Ted and I short ones, so when ours expired we threw ourselves at him. My fiancée looks after it,' he added. 'It's a bit crowded if we're lucky to get away together, but usually we can't. Why don't you come round one evening?'

She hesitated, and Timothy cut in.

'You most positively will. Second floor, windows protected against blast, excellent air-raid shelter downstairs, service A.1,' he insisted, and Julia laughed.

'All right—I'd love to, but I don't want to take you away from your friends. You haven't long.'

'Absolutely nothing to worry about,' said Timothy with enthusiasm. 'Ted and Pat have their ladies, and I'm tired of being odd man out.' They were in his compartment, and he pulled his luggage down from the rack, then opened the door for her. As she went through he winked at the others, and when he had disappeared, Ted looked with an eyebrow raised at Dawlish.

'I await results with curiosity.'

'They should be interesting,' said Pat. 'Oh, well, we'll see what happens in Town. We'll go to the flat first, as we might be followed. Then on to Room 13 in the black-out; following won't be so easy then.'

They were off the train before the others, and waited for them. Dawlish saw the hatless, dark-haired man a few yards behind Timothy and Julia Dawnay, but did not give him a thought. He did not see the passenger who stepped close to an electric luggage trolley and quickly and expertly release the brakes.

He heard the whine, looked round, and saw the trolley moving towards Tim.

Beresford saw it at the same time, and bellowed:

'Jump, Tim! Get away!'

But Dawlish had reached his friend and the woman, and with a sweeping lunge swept them out of the path of the oncoming trolley, which, passing within a few inches of them crashed against a pile of luggage.

Shakily, the lady who had both lingered and lured straightened up, to find Timothy brushing down his trousers, and Dawlish looking at her in some concern.

'I'm awfully sorry,' he said. 'I hope you're all right.'

'I—yes, of course,' she said.

But she was not. She was frightened. He could see fear in her violet eyes, and in the way her lips trembled for a moment before she regained control over herself. She looked quickly about the platform, and suddenly he saw her expression stiffen. As if looking for Ted, he turned his head, to see who it was who had riveted her attention.

For the first time he saw the man with red hair.

CHAPTER FOUR

THE MAN WITH RED HAIR

Dawlish would have noticed him in any case.

The hair, thick and growing upwards stiffly, ended in a quiff which apparently refused to lie down. Its owner was a man of medium height with the peculiarly creamy complexion of the red haired, and a pair of very piercing blue eyes. They were looking intently at Julia Dawnay.

The man and the woman stared at each other for some seconds, while Dawlish said casually to Beresford:

'Are you all right, old son?'

'No damage at all,' said Ted. 'By Jingo, you moved! Who the deuce let that truck get out of control?'

'Some idiot of a porter,' said Dawlish confidently. He was in time to see Red Hair getting into a low-lying car which had a chauffeur at the wheel. It was in his mind to suggest that Beresford followed him, but he hesitated because of the difficulty of doing so without Julia Dawnay hearing him; and in any case, the car disappeared so quickly that following would have been useless. Dawlish turned back to Julia.

'It really doesn't matter,' she was saying, 'but it did scare me.'

'It scared me, too. I've half a mind to make a fuss about it. It was criminal carelessness.'

'Please don't,' said Julia quickly.

Though he was not quite certain of it himself, Dawlish saw that she had no doubt at all that there had been a deliberate attempt to run her down; there could be no other reason for the fear he had seen in her eyes. She would not have lost her poise so completely because of an accident.

He said easily to Tim:

'You two get off, and we'll see you at the flat later. We're relying on you coming round one evening,' he added to Julia, and extended his hand. Her answering grip was quick and firm.

Dawlish was left with the impression that she wanted to say something else, but whatever it was she kept it to herself. She smiled at them out of the taxi window, while Beresford was saying:

'What was it, Pat?'

'Dirty work,' said Dawlish promptly, 'or I've missed my guess. I now make restitution.' He turned to a muttering and disgruntled porter who had overheard much that had passed.

'What's your name?' asked Dawlish unexpectedly.

'What's that got ter do with you?'

'As witness to an accident you might be needed,' said Dawlish amiably, and he smiled at the man. The transformation when Dawlish smiled was an amazing thing; it worked miracles with women, and—it was often said—inspired confidence in men. The porter was no exception.

'I blamed one of you fellows for it,' Dawlish went on, 'but I remember now that the trolley was standing unattended. I don't want to give a wrong impression when I report it.'

'When you—*oh-oh*, a noospaper man, eh?' The half-crown that Dawlish handed him proved fairly effective. After announcing that his name was Jo Whipple, the man claimed that he had seen a fellow touch the trolley.

'Can you be quite sure?' asked Dawlish.

'I got eyes, ain't I? There's a lot of them abaht—they can't leave nuthing alone. Gotta see how it works.' It was evident that Jo Whipple had a grudge against passengers as a whole, and the curious type in particular.

'Would you recognize him again?' asked Dawlish.

'Reckernize him anywhere,' said Jo. 'I see him going to the trolley an' I ses, that's one of them, I ses, I ses it to George, who's gorn over to Number 1 platform. I ses if he touches that ruddy truck I'll knock his block off, I ses, and then someone gives me a job, and as soon as I turn me head off she goes.'

'Who gave you the job?' asked Dawlish.

'Red-haired cove,' said Jo Whipple simply.

Dawlish was more than interested; he was impressed. The porter had been watching a man by the truck, and Red Hair had given him a trunk to carry, thus making it impossible for Jo to maintain that watch. It suggested a degree of organization and quick thinking which was more than casual; and it was further evidence that the trolley had been deliberately set in motion to run Julia Dawnay down.

'I see,' said Dawlish at last. 'Jo, if you see the man who started that truck again, can you find out anything about him?'

'Wotjer mean, find out anything?'

'Name, address, destination,' said Dawlish.

'No, I can't,' said Jo with emphasis. 'Here, what are you, a newspaperman or a copper?' His eyes watched Dawlish's hand, as Dawlish extracted from his wallet a one pound note. When it had changed hands he said grudgingly: 'I *might* be able to find where he was goin', an' if he had a case I could look at the label. Have their addresses on them, some do. How's that?'

Dawlish added his card to the pound note.

'If you find out his name and address, Jo, telephone me and I'll make it another pound. But it's strictly between you and me, you understand. Have you seen him before?'

'Happen I have, two or three times. Once last week—week ago Monday. Going up to Scotland he was, had a sleeper on the night train.'

'A week ago on Monday,' said Dawlish thoughtfully. 'That might be useful. Well, keep this to yourself, there's a good fellow, and wish me luck when you have a drink.' He smiled and rejoined Beresford, who was standing by their kit and looking gloomily about him. But as Dawlish drew near he spoke softly:

'The station's haunted, Pat.'

'You look enough to haunt anyone,' said Dawlish. 'Who by?'

'I don't know.' Beresford was serious. 'Everywhere I look I'm watched. There's a cove over by the bookstall pretending to read a paper. Another fellow by a taxi. Another by the train. A fourth by a trolley.'

Casually Dawlish looked about him.

He saw a pair of eyes drop beneath a newspaper, another looked suddenly in a different direction, a third returned his gaze insolently. There was no mistake: they were being watched, and it was an uncanny feeling.

'We'll walk to the exit,' he said.

As they went out of the station a cab pulled up in front of them.

'Cab, sir?' asked the driver.

He was an old man with grey hair that needed cutting, and he wore a pair of steel-rimmed glasses mended at two places by black cotton. Dawlish shook his head curtly, and stepped across the road to a line of cabs for hire.

The driver of the first was sitting at the wheel reading a sporting paper. He tucked it away and leaned out to open the door. The mild-looking cabby on the other side of the road was staring, and Dawlish thought that his gaze was particularly intense; that might, of course, be solely because the man had been passed over.

'Ted,' he said, 'take the next cab. Follow that fellow over there if he moves.'

A second cab had drawn up behind the mild driver and into it climbed two men who had been watching them on the platform. It all worked so smoothly and casually that it seemed genuinely coincidental: neither Dawlish nor Beresford would have thought anything of it had they not been on the alert. But as Beresford's cab began to move, that into which the watchers had climbed followed Dawlish's.

The mild driver, although without a fare, followed Beresford.

Dawlish looked back through the small rear window as they turned a corner. He was not smiling; there had been times when he might have found this surveillance amusing, but for the moment he disliked it intensely. Why should he be followed? How had anyone learned that he had been summoned on a mysterious errand—so mysterious that he himself did not know what it was about?

He reached Jermyn Street without incident, and his driver stopped at Number 88g. The cab behind him passed by; Ted's drew up, and the mild driver with the steel spectacles also passed by.

The two large men paid off their cabbies, and regarded each other on the threshold of the house. Very slowly Ted shook his head.

'I don't believe it,' he said.

'I'm beginning to agree with you,' said Dawlish. 'However, we'll go in. I wonder if Felicity's there?' He had wired to her before leaving Doncaster, but he could not be sure that the wire would arrive ahead of him.

There was no lift, and he walked quickly up to the second floor. He wished that there had been no Julia Dawnay, no red-haired man, no mysterious affair on the platform, no convoy of cabbies. He wanted to see Felicity, to talk and laugh with her, hug her, feast his eyes on her. Everything else was an unwonted distraction.

He did not use his key, but rang the front-door bell. Ted put his luggage down and they waited, but before the door opened they heard the murmur of voices, and Dawlish recognized Felicity's.

'I tell you that he's not expected,' she was saying. 'It's quite useless to wait.'

The voice which answered her was cultured and even mellow, yet there was something in its timbre which Dawlish disliked. He scowled, for he had put two and two together and he was assuming that someone had called to see him, knowing he would arrive, although Felicity had not yet received his telegram. He waited impatiently for the door to open, and then he saw her, tall and slim, neither dark nor fair. Her green-grey eyes, in his opinion the loveliest eyes in creation, widened when she saw him; her well-shaped lips parted in an exclamation of delight.

'Pat! Darling!' Quite unperturbed by Ted or the man behind her she flung her arms about his neck, and for a moment he held her tight. She was so vital, everything she did and said was so exactly as he knew it would be. She drew back. 'It *is* you.'

'Of course,' said the man with the cultured voice, and he

stepped into Dawlish's line of vision. 'I told you that he would come, Miss Deverall. How do you do, Captain Dawlish?'

Dawlish did not immediately answer; for the second time he was looking at the man with red hair.

CHAPTER FIVE

DAWLISH IS ABRUPT

Dawlish put an arm about Felicity's shoulder, and went forward with her into the room. She sensed something of his tension, and her face lost its brightness, and her expression grew sober. Beresford followed them.

'I think you have the advantage of me,' said Dawlish evenly.

'I believe I do.' The red-haired man took a card from his pocket and handed it to Dawlish, who did not immediately look at it. Instead he regarded the visitor. It was difficult to assess his age: Dawlish put him at between forty and fifty, and left it at that. The most remarkable things about him were his red hair and his piercing blue eyes. He did not look a man easily put at a disadvantage.

Dawlish looked at the card, and read:

Mr. Sebastian Bray

There was no address, and no telephone number.

'So you are Mr. Bray,' said Dawlish more easily. 'And you seem to be well acquainted with me. You still have the advantage, you know my address.'

Bray smiled. 'My own address is so uncertain that I'm not sure you are right,' he said. 'But at the moment I am staying at the Clarion Hotel. If you should wish to get in touch with me you will find me there for a day or two.'

Not by a flicker of an eyelid did Dawlish show that the Clarion Hotel meant anything to him. Beresford cleared his throat noisily.

'Why should I wish to get in touch with you?'

'It's a possibility,' said Bray suavely, 'that might be considered. May I have the pleasure of a few minutes with you alone, Captain Dawlish?'

'Quite unnecessary,' said Dawlish bluntly. 'What you have to say can be said here, and now.'

Bray's eyebrows rose in surprise rather than affront, and he shrugged his shoulders.

'As you like. Captain Dawlish—'

'We know who I am,' said Dawlish, and Felicity knew that he was deliberately trying to anger the visitor.

'You appear to be wilfully uncivil,' said Bray, 'but again that is for you to decide. You are in London on special leave, and you will be asked to interest yourself in a matter which is not strictly in your sphere. I want to remind you that under the terms of your commission you are not bound to obey orders other than those confined to military matters. Is that not the case?'

'Anyone familiar with the King's Regulations should know,' said Dawlish.

'Precisely, Captain Dawlish. I want to impress upon you the need for acting in a most circumspect manner within the next week or ten days. I strongly recommend that you refuse any suggestion of operating outside the sphere for which you are contracted. Is that quite clear?'

'There are quite a number of things that are quite clear,' said Dawlish coldly. 'Sit down, Mr. Bray.'

'Thank you, but that is all I have to say.'

'Sit down,' said Dawlish slowly.

His eyes met Bray's; there was a moment of hesitation, and then the red-haired man obeyed. Dawlish put one hand in his pocket, and leaned against a chair. Beresford was sitting in another, Felicity, who had uttered no further word, stood near the door. She was frowning a little; the joy of the meeting had gone.

'May I in my turn,' said Dawlish drily, 'impress upon you the foolishness of this visit? The inference is very clear that you are in possession of information that should be beyond your sphere.' His lips curled a little; clearly he did not like Sebastian Bray. 'How did you learn it?'

'That is entirely my business.'

'Before you leave here it will be mine,' said Dawlish.

The other's eyes narrowed; Felicity breathed rather more quickly, and Beresford crossed one leg over the other.

'I don't think you quite understand,' said Bray softly. 'I should not have come here had I not been quite sure that I could handle any emergency. My aim was to make an amicable arrangement with you. After all, Captain Dawlish, you are away from London for a long time. Miss Deverall is here on her own, and in these difficult days accidents are so easily met.'

Dawlish moved then.

He was resting against the chair one moment, and he was in front of Sebastian Bray the next. His right hand shot out, pulling the man from the chair as easily as he would a child.

Dawlish kept him like that for some seconds, and then deliberately let him fall back in the chair.

'You have narrowly escaped a violent end,' he said. He spoke as if he meant it, and Bray's eyes showed something akin to fear. There was utter silence in the room for some seconds, and then Beresford said in a voice both gay and flippant.

'I'm hungry.'

Bray turned and stared at him, as he might at a half-wit.

'Good idea,' Dawlish said easily. 'Any luck in the flat, darling, or will we have to go out?' He lit a cigarette. 'Fortnum's will be able to let us have something, won't they?'

'I'll see what there is in the larder, and then 'phone them.' Felicity walked between Dawlish and Bray, stretching out a hand and touching Pat's hand as she passed. 'What a lousy journey it was,' Dawlish said. 'I wonder how long Tim will be.'

Bray stared from one to the other. His collar and shirt front were rumpled and his coat was rucked up, but the noticeable thing about him was the frustration in his eyes. He looked bewildered, as if he were in a world unfamiliar and frightening. He cleared his throat as Beresford said:

'Felicity's looking grand. Good to be home again, my son. Ten days of rest and ease—'

'And then back to the Army to sleep it off,' grinned Dawlish.

Sebastian Bray cleared his throat again. For the first time since Beresford had spoken Dawlish looked at him, with an easy contemplative smile on his lips.

'Hallo,' he said, 'have you come round?'

'Dawlish—'

'Yes?'

'You are making one of the mistakes of your life.'

'That's a matter of opinion,' said Dawlish; 'my own view is that the shoe is on the other foot. I might well have carted you to the police before you came round. As it is I'll be lenient and telephone them.'

'You'll—*what?*'

'Telephone the police. Tell them that there is a stranger here who knows Army facts which he should not. In such circumstances I doubt your popularity very much.'

'What are we waiting for?' demanded Beresford.

'Don't be an ass,' said Dawlish, tartly. 'Felicity will want to get through to Fortnum's first. I'm hungry, and ten minutes makes no difference one way or the other. Or does it?' he asked amiably of Sebastian Bray.

'You—you're mad,' said Bray.

'Possibly. However—'

He broke off as Felicity came out of the kitchen and went to the telephone, calling a food store. When she finished Dawlish took her place and dialled Whitehall 1212.

'Are you calling the police?' Bray asked sharply.

'I am. Worried?' asked Dawlish. 'After all, I have your word for it that you wouldn't come here without being quite sure that you could handle any emergency, so here's a chance to prove it.' He raised the receiver. 'Hallo . . . Chief Inspector Trivett, please . . . all right, if he's not in give me Sir Archibald Morely . . . The Assistant Commissioner, that's right . . . eh? . . . Dawlish, Captain Patrick Dawlish.'

He finished, holding the receiver to his ear and regarding his visitor. There had not been a moment's doubt in his mind as to the way he should act, but he was surprised to see that Bray now showed every sign of self-possession. After a short pause a voice reached his ear from Scotland Yard.

'The Assistant Commissioner speaking,' said Sir Archibald Morely sharply. 'Who is that?'

'Who else but Dawlish?' said Dawlish amiably. 'Archie, I've a peculiar specimen for you here.'

Morely's voice grew irritable: 'Oh it's you, is it. Where are you speaking from? I thought you were up in some godforsaken place in the north.'

'I almost wish I were,' said Dawlish, and then he went on soberly: 'Seriously, old man, I came down from the north under secret orders, and this chappie seems to know all about them. Come and look after him for me, will you, or send some of those men of yours.'

Morely hesitated.

'Are you joking, Pat?'

'My dear man, I've never been more serious. His name's Bray. I can't give you his address, but—what's that?'

Morely said sharply: 'What did you say his name was?'

'Bray.'

'Is he red haired?' asked Morely, still sharply.

Dawlish frowned. 'Yes, he is.'

'What have you done to him?' snapped Morely.

'Very little yet,' said Dawlish slowly, and when he looked across the room he saw that Bray was smiling; it was not a pleasant smile. 'I've shaken him up once for careless talk, that's all.'

'Oh, my Lord!' exclaimed Morely. 'Pat, don't play any of your fool tricks with Bray. Let him go at once. No, don't argue about it, let him go.'

'Are you *serious*?' Dawlish demanded.

'Of course I'm serious. And don't ask me to explain. Let him go, and if you're wise you'll apologize to him. Sorry to be mysterious, Pat, but I can't help it. You just mustn't manhandle Bray.'

Very clearly the telephone went down in Morely's office, and very blankly Dawlish stared across the room at Sebastian Bray, who was smiling widely as he stepped towards the chair where his hat and gloves were lying.

CHAPTER SIX

ROOM 13

'Just a moment,' said Dawlish slowly.

Bray by then was at the door, and his hand was on the latch. He turned as Dawlish spoke, one eyebrow raised a little above the other. Dawlish was trying to get the matter into focus, but it was not easy. Not only had Morely been definite and almost alarmed, but Bray had *expected* to be released. It was quite absurd: but it had happened.

Dawlish, however, was not easily frustrated. He had come to a decision as Bray reached the door, and as he spoke he gave an almost imperceptible nod to Beresford. Beresford eased himself from his chair and went towards Bray: the red-haired man stiffened.

'You had instructions,' he snapped. 'Act on them.'

Dawlish grinned.

'You've forgotten King's Regulations,' he said. 'I'm a soldier now. In peace I might have taken Scotland Yard advice, in war I think others should be consulted. Sit down again, Mr. Bray.'

'I shall do nothing of the kind. I warned you just now of the possible consequences of stubbornness on your part. That warning still holds good. I have the full confidence of the authorities. My visit here was out of consideration for yourself, and nothing more. If you are foolish enough to ignore it, you will find yourself in difficulties. You have received instructions from the Assistant Commissioner himself, I gather. You will receive the same instructions from anyone else in authority whom you approach, and unless you are careful you will be severely reprimanded. Be advised, Captain Dawlish.'

Dawlish eyed him evenly.

Beresford was near enough to Bray to prevent him making a move to open the door. Felicity sat back in a chair, her cooking neglected. She did not feel so much afraid as on edge.

She had disliked the red-haired man on sight.

She had, however, been as much puzzled by him as worried. Why should a man talk in a manner intended to frighten Pat, when—if he had any knowledge of Pat at all—he would realize that by his threat he had merely hardened him into enmity? Dawlish might have tolerated Bray's manner, his suave innuendos, his calm effrontery: but the talk of danger to herself he could not and would not forgive.

Several facts passed through Dawlish's mind; he was detached and not personally perturbed, but Morely's manner and Bray's confidence puzzled him. He disliked being puzzled; he disliked the peculiar circumstances of the past twelve hours, but that did not prevent him from considering his final attitude towards Bray.

He believed Bray when the man said that he would receive similar instructions if he approached the military authorities: Morely must have been quite sure of himself before he had talked as he had. But in Dawlish there was a streak of obstinacy allied to a firm belief that, capable and comprehensive though the police were, there were occasions when they were too tightly bound by conventional rules; the same could be said of the War Office.

Dawlish, in normal life, appeared the most conventional of men. He dressed the right way and lived or stayed in the right places; he ate and drank those things that a young man about town should eat and drink; he had a mild fund of risque stories; he knew all the night-clubs and where one could gamble moderately while safe from the police; his conversation, if not brilliant, was passable. He was reasonably wealthy, he had the *entree* to virtually any house in London where his own kind forgathered: but in truth there was nothing conventional beneath his well-assumed normalcy.

The pertinent facts passed slowly through his mind.

Bray's knowledge of his 'secret' orders might easily be explained; Bray's visit here could even—with a stretch of imagination—be explained. But the threats, and the affair at the station, could not be explained so easily. It was clearly possible for the man to act and talk as he had and feel quite immune from the police, but just as certainly such immunity was unjustifiable. If the police refused to do anything about it, then—thought Dawlish—the police were in error. Dawlish was in no way bound to the police as such; when he had co-operated with them he had often acted in a way directly contrary to their methods and their regulations; he did not want to work with them, but if he did, it would be in his own way.

Thus thought Dawlish.

'Have you finished thinking?' demanded Bray, and his voice was a sneer.

'Not quite,' said Dawlish amiably. 'I haven't decided where to put you, Mr. Sebastian Bray. Have you a liking for any particular part of the country?'

Bray's piercing eyes blazed.

'Don't talk to me like that! I am going!' He turned towards the door, but as he stretched out a hand Beresford's large fingers closed about his wrist. Bray tried to free himself, but it was like trying to escape from handcuffs. He pushed at Beresford; he might as successfully have pushed against a stone wall.

'Now, now,' said Dawlish. 'Temper won't get you anywhere, little man. I am merely going to let you have a short holiday, where you can cool your heels and, I hope, revise your opinion of yourself.'

Bray went very still. His words, when they came were high and venomous.

'Dawlish, if you do not immediately have me released, I shall—I shall—' his glance shot significantly towards Felicity.

Dawlish did not this time rise to the bait.

'Your mistake,' he said mildly. 'In fact that has been your mistake from the beginning. All right, Ted.'

He did not need to say what was all right. Beresford did not release Bray's right wrist, but struck him quickly on the point of the jaw. It was a short arm jab which had just the requisite strength: it snapped Bray's teeth together, and it put him out on his feet. Beresford caught and carried him to the couch as if he were used to doing it every day of the week.

'Now you've committed yourself,' he said.

'Pat, you shouldn't,' said Felicity from the door.

Dawlish smiled at her.

'You may be right, darling, but I'm taking a chance for the time being at least. I dislike Mr. Bray. I dislike the influence which Mr. Bray appears to exert. I think we might act in a strictly private way for the time being, don't you?'

Felicity hesitated; his eyes seemed to ask her for her trust; she had never seriously considered keeping it back.

'I don't want you to run into trouble,' she said.

'Certainly not,' said Dawlish cheerfully. 'It ran into me.' He regarded the prostrate form of Sebastian Bray with keen interest, and mused: 'There's only one place to take him, I think. Pinky will back us up. Have you seen him lately, Fel?'

'He was up for a few days,' said Felicity.

'The old reprobate,' grinned Dawlish. 'He lives fifty miles from danger, but has to come up to Town to see what it's like.' He looked at his watch. 'It's half-past five, and we ought to be away by eight o'clock for the Clarion. Let's get him tied up, and we can worry about him then.'

With the help of cord from the kitchen, a handkerchief, and some sticking-plaster, they bound and gagged Sebastian Bray. As the two men worked, Felicity made a half-hearted beginning at the grill, but she was frequently at the door to watch progress. Pat smiled round at her.

'I've been looking forward to one of your grills for six months,' he said, 'but we'll postpone it, darling. Ring the restaurant for a snack.'

Although there were only four flats in that building, other houses in Jermyn Street were also converted into flats, and on the ground floor of one of them was a restaurant which serviced the whole row of buildings. Felicity rang up with alacrity, and as she came from the telephone Bray opened his eyes.

'There's only one thing for it,' said Dawlish. 'You can take him down, Ted, and get back as soon as you can. I'll make your excuses. And it will be an idea, I think, if you take Felicity with you.'

'Where are you going?' Felicity demanded.

Dawlish smiled: 'I'll tell you in a few minutes. There's no need to let Bray hear everything; the gentleman knows too much already.'

Before the meal arrived there was a ring at the front door, and Tim Jeremy entered. His eyes were bright, and he gave the impression of being thoroughly pleased with himself. He beamed at Felicity, then regarded the prostrate figure of Sebastian Bray with some interest though no apparent concern.

'She's coming tomorrow,' he announced.

'Good work,' said Dawlish. 'Was the flat being watched?'

'I *did* notice a cove,' admitted Timothy.

'Where?'

'Sitting at the wheel of an Alvis. Chauffeur.'

'That's Bray's chauffeur,' said Dawlish thoughtfully. He hesitated as the waiter was heard approaching, diverted him to the dining-room, saw his departure, and then continued:

'We'll have this snack, and then we'll interview the chauffeur chappie. He may be the only man who knows where Bray is, and there seems to me no reason why he shouldn't keep his employer company.'

'No reason at all,' said Timothy languidly. 'Dare I ask what it's about, or doesn't that matter?'

Dawlish explained briefly. Tim gave a smile of considerable enjoyment.

'*Very* nice work,' he said. 'I couldn't have thought it out better myself. So Ted and Felicity take Bray and the chauffeur away—'

'In Bray's car,' said Beresford.

'While we see what's what,' said Tim. 'It's very neat, Pat, *very* neat. Felicity my sweet, is there any beer?'

'Of course there's beer,' said Felicity.

'Then fill 'em up,' said Tim. 'We'll drink to it.'

They drank soberly, to Sebastian Bray and all that he meant, and fell to on the meal. As they finished Dawlish turned to Tim:

'Better get your car out old chap, and follow Ted and Felicity. There might be someone following *them*. Both of you get back to the Clarion as soon as you can, and I'll tell whoever's there that you missed a train.'

'That suits me,' said Tim.

He went out five minutes afterwards, and Beresford took himself off to the bathroom for a shower. For the first time since he had arrived Dawlish was alone with Felicity. She turned to him, her eyes deeply clouded.

'Pat, you're sure it's all right?'

'I'm not a bit sure,' admitted Pat Dawlish, cheerfully, 'but there's nothing else we can do. If there are repercussions, we'll bluff our way out.' He hugged her. 'Game for it, darling?'

'Of course. But I wish it were clearer.'

'That will come,' said Dawlish. 'And now watch from the window Dawlish being clever.' He planted a kiss on the back of her neck, and went out.

In two minutes Felicity saw him walking towards the Alvis.

The big car was just in sight, and the chauffeur at the wheel was reading an evening paper. Dawlish appearing to saunter, without a care in the world, walked up to him, and stopped.

What they said she could not hear.

After a few seconds, the chauffeur climbed from his seat, and walked back with Dawlish to the house. Felicity hurried to open the door.

The chauffeur touched his hat.

Dawlish urged him through, and the door was closed. It was then that the man saw his employer. In an instant he moved his right hand towards his left shoulder.

Dawlish struck at him.

But Dawlish had under-estimated the man, who ducked, moving swiftly. A gun flashed from a shoulder-holster. Although he did not fire, it was clear that he would not take much prompting to do so. Felicity felt a sharp spasm of fear. The chauffeur was a short, wiry man with a swarthy face and hard brown eyes.

'Move from that door,' he ordered. 'Undo those cords, and be quick about it.' His voice held a trace of Cockney, and the impression that Dawlish had first had, of an Italian or a Spanish half-breed, strengthened. Not that Dawlish spent much time in wondering about the ancestry of the chauffeur with a gun.

Obediently he bent over the prisoner, touching the cords at Bray's hands.

CHAPTER SEVEN

THIRD VISITOR

Felicity watched, waiting.

She could not believe that Pat would let himself lose so easily. She had grown suddenly convinced that Pat was right, that the man on the couch should not be released no matter what the police ordered. A man who made threats and had for a chauffeur an expert gunman needed explaining.

But what would Dawlish do?

The hard brown eyes of the chauffeur were turned towards him, and the gun did not waver. From the bathroom came the sound of splashing water; Beresford could hear nothing of what was happening. Dawlish bent lower over the prisoner; and then he moved in a way which startled Felicity, and made the chauffeur curse.

He slid his hands under Bray and lifted him bodily from the couch. Swerving round, he tossed the man towards the pointing gun. As the chauffeur jumped to one side, Felicity picked up a book and hurled it at him. It caught him on the shoulder, and before he had recovered Dawlish's service revolver was in his hand.

'I'll take that gun, I think,' said Dawlish, and he wrested the automatic from the other, in a quick movement which seemed effortless. 'Turn round.'

The man hesitated, his eyes both watchful and dangerous.

Dawlish put out his free hand, and spun the chauffeur round; the man staggered, and would have fallen but for Dawlish's retaining grip. Felicity looked hopelessly across the room.

'How can you get *two* of them out?' she demanded.

'That's easy,' said Dawlish, 'we'll wait until after dark.' He moved his revolver in his hand, and struck the chauffeur on the nape of the neck; the man collapsed as quickly as Bray had done and Dawlish smiled grimly.

Working swiftly he gagged and bound the fallen man and dragged both him and Bray into the bedroom. The noise brought Beresford quickly on the scene. 'Sure we can get them away, Pat?'

'I don't see why not. There's no moon, and we can carry 'em or make them walk—they will, with a gun in their ribs. And no one will notice that they're gagged.'

Felicity looked on, a little bleakly. She had a blind faith in Dawlish, and it had to see her through. 'Well now,' he went on, 'you and Ted take the gentlemen to Pinky's, and Tim follows you to prevent accidents. I go to Room 13,' he added thoughtfully. 'I'm getting quite anxious to know more about it. Watch from the window again, darling; I'm going to take a stroll simply for the sake of it this time.'

He walked the length of Jermyn Street, enjoying the cool evening air. It would not grow dark until half-past seven, and he wished that the time would pass quickly; the sooner Bray and his man were away from Jermyn Street the happier he would be.

He saw no one who might be watching him, or the flat.

The people in the cabs, it seemed, had followed him and

Ted solely to make sure that they arrived at Jermyn Street. If, as Dawlish suspected, the watchers at the station had been on Bray's pay-roll, that was all they would want to know. He found himself thinking of Julia Dawnay, and he wondered whether someone who was working with her had looked through his luggage, or whether that had been an emissary from Bray.

There was, of course, no certainty that she had deliberately aimed to get their interest for any ulterior motive; but he thought it more than likely. He imagined that Julia Dawnay, who had a shop in Brake Street, could tell him a great deal.

Meanwhile he had to assess the other factors.

He was not working under direct orders; had he contacted with the War Office and been told to let Bray go he would have had no choice in the matter; there were, after all, limits to what he could take into his own hands. He had really overstepped that limit after the talk with Morely; but Morely had no jurisdiction over him. He had assaulted Bray but that could be answered— it was in self-defence; he smiled at that thought, although the gunman-chauffeur would support such an assertion.

Abduction was a different matter.

Dawlish had acted quickly, not on a sudden idea, however, but after deliberation. The police would do nothing to interrogate Bray: he was determined to.

He considered Pinky.

The full appellation of that gentleman was Sir Jeremiah Pinkerton, O.B.E. He was his uncle. More than that; Dawlish was the knight's only living relative, and his heir. Once before, Sir Jeremiah had assisted his nephew, outwardly against his will, actually with zest; he would again. But how far was Dawlish justified in implicating him?

Ted and Tim were less important; they could participate or not, as they wished, and he knew what they would wish. He was not pleased that Felicity had to be involved, and yet, thinking of Felicity, was like thinking of himself. His uncle was the man who had to be considered, and he could not easily get in touch with him; the telephones were not in good order in London, and long-distance calls were subject to a long delay. In any case, he could hardly go into details on the telephone. He smiled at the thought that Felicity could doubtless handle Pinky, and then he retraced his steps to the flat. No one was watching; he was quite sure of that.

Timothy's car was drawn up in front of Bray's Alvis, and in the flat Beresford had finished dressing. With Felicity and Tim he was holding a counsel of war. Comparing notes, they found that they regarded the thing in exactly the same light; until they learned more of Sebastian Bray, he must be kept out of circulation. That cheered Dawlish, who smiled when Felicity said:

'What would Trivett say?'

'My dear sweet girl, Trivett would be shocked to the core of his being,' said Dawlish. 'Chief Inspectors of Scotland Yard can't countenance such things. It wouldn't have surprised me,' he added, 'had Trivett been waiting for me here; I took it for granted when I heard we were all booked for the same adventure that the police were behind it, but Morely didn't give that impression, and Trivett hasn't arrived.' He looked at his watch. 'Six-fifteen, blast it. Doesn't it ever get dark?'

'We could take a chance now,' said Beresford.

'Don't be an ass. We can't carry two able-bodied men out in broad daylight, and we certainly can't take 'em out at the point of a gun. Well, I'm going to have a bath, folk, it will while away the time.'

Dusk was falling by the time he had finished. It was a quarter to seven, and Dawlish thought that by a quarter past it would be dark enough for them to venture to the cars.

At seven o'clock precisely there was a ring at the front door bell. They stared at each other, and that instinctive movement was an indication of what they were feeling. Felicity jumped up.

'I'll go,' she said.

Dawlish let her, but went after her, standing by the lounge door in a position where he could see who was outside. Felicity opened the door.

On the threshold was no less a person that Chief Inspector William Trivett of the C.I.D.

Dawlish stepped swiftly back into the lounge, and closed the door which communicated with the bedroom. Beresford and Jeremy stared but asked no questions, while from the hall came Felicity's voice.

'Hallo, Inspector, it's nice to see you.' Bless her! thought Dawlish fervently; she could put up an act with anyone. 'You know that he's home, then?'

'I had heard,' said Trivett drily.

He entered the lounge, a tall, spare man, dark and well-dressed. He walked with the easy step of the athlete, and he was smiling a little as he saw Dawlish, Beresford and Jeremy leaning back in their chairs. Dawlish beamed at him, and rose slowly to his feet.

'Well, well, well!' he said. 'This is a welcome with a vengeance. How are things, William?'

'Hallo, Pat.' Trivett shook hands all round, and Dawlish felt a little relieved; Trivett was not here on an unpleasant errand—at least not one which was too unpleasant, or he would have been more formal; he did not willingly mix business with pleasure. 'Quite a coincidence, isn't it?'

'What is?' asked Dawlish innocently.

'You three on leave together. How did you manage it?'

'It was managed for us,' said Dawlish, stepping towards the cocktail cabinet. 'What will you drink?'

'Beer, thanks,' said Trivett, and he chatted with Ted and the others while Felicity and Pat filled the tankards.

'Here's how!'

'To the police force!'

'May it grow wings!'

Putting his tankard down, Trivett eyed Dawlish with a certain gravity. 'Pat,' he said, 'what are you up to?'

'We-ell,' said Dawlish judicially. 'Each and everyone of us had notice to get to London quickly, and to report. Don't you know anything about it?'

Trivett said clearly.

'I do not. I was quite happy to think you were away from London and not running your fool heads into trouble. Seriously, what *are* you doing?'

'You know as much as we do,' said Dawlish.

Trivett looked dubious, and appealed to Felicity.

'Is he telling the truth, do you know?'

'If he isn't he lied to me,' said Felicity, sitting on the arm of Pat's chair. 'You wouldn't do that, darling, would you?' She entwined a strand of his hair about her finger.

'I'd rather lie to Trivett,' said Dawlish in mock anguish, 'so there's no need to pull. We're the folk to ask questions, Bill. I rang Morely up an hour or so ago—has he gone loco?'

Trivett was serious.

'He has not. That's really what I'm here about—he told me to have a friendly word with you. Whatever you do, Pat, don't get yourselves mixed up with Sebastian Bray. That's essential. I had an uncomfortable feeling that he might still be here,' added Trivett, looking idly about the room.

'My dear man!' exclaimed Dawlish. 'After the sacrosanct

person of the Assistant Commissioner told me to let him go? I'm surprised at you. But seriously, what's the mystery about the gentleman? His manner and his knowledge were alike unpleasant. As a matter of fact if Felicity hadn't persuaded me I would have held him until I'd had time for a talk with you.'

Beresford and Jeremy maintained straight faces, and Felicity said sweetly:

'My influence is growing, you see.'

'I hope it keeps growing,' said Trivett grimly. 'Bray is not a man to antagonize at the moment.' Dawlish was puzzled by the qualification inherent in 'at the moment' but said nothing, while the others hid their growing concern. Trivett went on: 'He's over here as an envoy from Ireland—Eire, I should say. Not political—trade and economics. He has pretty well a *carte blanche* from the Dail, and we've got to treat the beggar to an orgy of appeasement. The Ministry of Information,' added Trivett with a touch of bitterness, 'is giving him a fanfare of radio trumpets tonight. I hope you haven't upset him, Pat. It will create a nasty situation if he turns sour. Just what did you do to him?'

CHAPTER EIGHT

THIN ICE

The only sign of Dawlish's feeling was that he stubbed out a ciga-rette before it was half-finished. Beresford and Tim maintained blank faces.

Felicity said unexpectedly: 'I wish they'd knocked his head off, the brute. Ugh!'

Trivett looked at her in surprise.

'Was he really as bad as that?'

'He was worse,' said Felicity, so forcibly that her listeners were able to relax a little, and even to smile. 'And I'll guarantee one thing,' she added, 'and that is that he's no more Irish than you are!'

The dangerous moment had passed. As Ted collected the tankards for refilling, Dawlish put in mildly:

'He didn't look particularly Irish to me, either. Are you *quite* sure that he's an envoy from Eire? He talked more like a top-drawer thug.'

'Just how?' asked Trivett.

'We-ell, he had a chauffeur with a gun. And he made unpleasing threats against Felicity. He knew—or guessed—that

I was in Town on a mystery mission, which he does not want me to take up. He even went as far as to tell me that I was not bound to act beyond the King's Regulations. In fact, Bill, if Morely hadn't been so uncompromising I would have kept both he and his chauffeur here.'

'How do you know the chauffeur had a gun?'

'I felt his left shoulder,' said Dawlish shamelessly. 'He carried a holster. If you'd said he was an I.R.A. agitator I wouldn't have been surprised.'

Trivett looked worried, but made it plain that he was not going to be communicative.

'I haven't been impressed by him myself,' he said, 'but you can take it for a fact that he's what he says he is. His identity has been checked beyond all doubt. As a matter of fact,' he went on, taking a folded evening paper from his pocket, 'his photograph's in here.'

The three thin leaves of the war-time evening paper were unfolded. The 'Sebastian Bray' story was in double-column head lines, and there was a reasonably good photograph of Bray: allowing for the blurred outlines, identification was not difficult.

'That's the fellow,' admitted Dawlish, and read:

ENVOY FROM EIRE IN LONDON

Great hopes are entertained in Whitehall of closer collaboration with Eire as a result of the visit of Eire's special envoy, Mr. Sebastian Bray, who arrived in England this morning. Mr. Bray is expected to stay in London for three or four days before returning to Dublin by air. He . . .

There was a great deal more, but Dawlish did not read it. He handed the paper to Tim.

'Well, all I can say is, that he didn't *behave* like a diplomat, Bill. Will you take this as a formal statement, or shall I write one out and send it along?' Dawlish asked.

'Do that,' said Trivett. 'Make it as full as you can. What terms were you on when he went?'

'Unpleasant,' said Dawlish promptly.

'You didn't manhandle him, did you?'

'Not as much as I wanted to.'

'That might mean anything,' said Trivett slowly. 'Oh, well, if he behaved as you say he did, there was excuse enough, I suppose, and he isn't likely to want it published that he took up any kind of arbitrary attitude with you. It will blow over. But keep clear of him, Pat. What's this job you've been called up for?'

'I don't know. Probably to start a training school for the A.T.S.,' said Dawlish with well-assumed bitterness. 'Bill, have you told me all you came to say?'

'Every word,' said Trivett, standing up. 'But I'll add that you had the Assistant Commissioner worried.'

'Well, if you say so. What are you busy on just now?'

Trivett smiled a little crookedly.

'From tomorrow morning onwards I shall be the personal bodyguard of Sebastian Bray,' he said. 'He wouldn't have one tonight—he said that he had some private matters to discuss, and that his chauffeur would look after him. Don't take too much notice of the shoulder-holster, Pat.' He shook hands all round, and some twenty minutes after his arrival the door closed on him.

Dawlish, Beresford and Timothy stood in silence. Felicity faced them with considerable spirit.

'Well,' she said sharply. 'I hope you're pleased with yourselves.'

'Before Trivett came you were on our side,' Dawlish said a little plaintively.

'I suppose there's no way of smoothing him down before he goes?' suggested Tim.

'Let *who* go?' Dawlish demanded.

'Bray, of course. You can't hold him now.'

'Obviously what Trivett said must alter things,' urged Beresford.

Dawlish pushed a hand through his hair and regarded them each in turn, and with some humour. He sat back in a chair and drummed his fingers on the arm, and then he said slowly:

'Until I've been to Room 13, our Sebastian remains tied up, and so does his chauffeur. He arranged to be free from police watchdogs until nine o'clock tomorrow morning, so we're all right until then.'

'All *what*?' demanded Ted.

'You're crazy,' said Tim, his melancholy face reflecting the depth of depression which the development had brought. 'You'll throw a spanner into the works which Whitehall's been trying to get moving since the war started. The Lord knows Bray will probably raise Cain now. What he'd be like after another twelve hours I daren't think.'

'I wonder,' said Felicity slowly, 'if another twelve hours *will* make all that difference.'

'You're the only one with a ha'porth of common sense,' said Dawlish smiling at her. 'If Bray—or perhaps I should say if the man who calls himself Bray—is really all that he pretends to be and all that Trivett makes out, he'll be in no sweeter temper now than he will be in the morning. Keeping him over-night will mean precisely nothing. Or at least, no more than we can handle.' He paused, and Felicity had the impression that he was thoroughly enjoying himself.

'We've two lines of argument,' continued Dawlish. 'One, that we believed this Bray to be an impostor. It could even be a fact, although I doubt it. If the four of us insisted on it, it might well avert any real nasty repercussions.'

'Except that if he *is* Bray—and of course he is,' said Tim gloomily, 'he won't be in a pleasant frame of mind for negotiating with our johnnies in the morning.'

'That wouldn't be the first diplomatic failure at Whitehall,' said Dawlish. 'But don't be so sure. Mr. Bray might be persuaded. He clearly believes in fear as a weapon, and that type often get scared very easily. The whole show is a fantastic lot of nonsense,' Dawlish added more sharply. 'Right's right, and I don't give a damn for diplomacy. Bray came here and talked like a crook— all right, we'll treat him like a crook.'

'Oh, well,' said Tim. 'They can't do more than court-martial us. I wonder what it will be like to be reduced to the ranks.'

'What a jolly little pessimist it is,' said Ted pleasantly. 'Actually I think Pat's right. Bray's a rogue. We'll have to prove it, but we've got twelve hours.'

'Well, are you all prepared to take the chance?'

'Count me in,' said Ted.

'And me,' said Tim gloomily.

Felicity nodded.

'Grand!' exclaimed Dawlish. 'But we've got to revise our plans. Obviously we can't take the bods to Hampshire, if we have to deliver them all nicely spitted and polished in the morning. But I don't want to keep them here.' He went to the telephone, was connected with the night-manager of the flats, and asked:

'Is there a furnished flat empty, do you know? Just for a night—I've some friends here unexpectedly.'

'Just a moment, sir—you'll want a ground-floor flat, I suppose?'

'It would be an advantage,' said Dawlish.

'I won't keep you a moment . . . yes, there's a ground floor flat at Number 16a. It's not in your block I'm afraid, sir, but it's only a walk of a hundred yards or so. Will that do?'

'Excellently,' said Dawlish. 'I'll take it for a week—is that all right?'

'You needn't do that, sir, we're always glad to help our tenants where we can. A night can easily be arranged.'

'All right,' said Dawlish. 'We'll make it a night, and I'll call you in the morning if we want to extend it. Don't have the people there called,' he added, 'they're in need of a rest.'

'I quite understand, sir. I'll send the key up to you right away. That is Mr. Jeremy speaking?'

'That's right,' said Dawlish. 'Thanks a lot.'

He rang down and eyed Jeremy with a grin:

'You've taken another flat for the night,' he said, 'and the manager thinks that you're leaving the straight and narrow path.'

'He isn't far wrong,' said Tim Jeremy sourly.

'It's a good idea,' said Felicity. 'How do you always manage to think of something?'

'Hark at her,' said Ted Beresford. 'She'll be telling him he's the only man in the world soon. This is no place for us.' He grinned. 'Do we take our guests along right away?'

'Slip down and make sure there's no one watching, if you can,' said Dawlish, jumping briskly to his feet, 'and as soon as the key comes we'll get moving.'

The key arrived in ten minutes, and in twenty-five Bray and his chauffeur were in a small, windowless room at Number 16a Jermyn Street. The two men had been conscious, and had walked—with coercion—along Jermyn Street. It was a pitch-dark night, and the only three people they had met passed quickly by, unaware of anything unusual.

As Dawlish shut the door of 16a, Ted drew a deep breath.

'Well, that's another rope cut, Pat. I thought you'd have a word with the beggar before you came away.'

'Let him get thoroughly worried,' said Dawlish. 'He'll be easier to talk to afterwards. Now we'll collect Felicity and get along to the Clarion right away.'

'Ought we to take a fourth?' asked Beresford.

'She isn't coming to Room 13, idiot,' said Dawlish, 'but I'd rather she was near us than on her own at the flat. I don't like any of the things that have so far happened, and I don't propose to let Felicity take any chances.'

In another ten minutes they bundled into Timothy's car; Bray's Alvis was left outside the flat after a word with the policeman on duty, who said that it would be all right there for an hour or two. A silent party, with Tim driving, reached the Clarion, in Piccadilly, and went through the blacked-out revolving doors.

Dawlish stepped to the reception desk, and asked for Room 13.

'What name, sir, please?'

'Captains Dawlish, Beresford and Jeremy.'

'That's all right, sir.' The clerk took a key from the row behind him.

'Thanks,' said Dawlish.

He took the key, and joined the others. As luck would have it, Felicity saw some friends sitting in the lounge. She made her way over to them while Dawlish left her with a lighter heart.

'Room 13, please,' he said to a page-boy, and the youngster took them to the first floor.

All three men were on tenterhooks, although none of them showed it, as the page-boy tapped at the door of Room 13.

They went through, to find a dining-table set for dinner,

round which three men and a woman were standing. The woman, poised, self-possessed, looking even lovelier than when they had last seen her, turned to greet them.

It was Julia Dawnay.

CHAPTER NINE

PROPOSITION

Dawlish recovered first.

Gravely taking the extended hand he met with smiling humour the limpid gaze of those violet eyes that had so intrigued him on the train.

'So, we meet again.'

Before she could answer, one of the men spoke.

He was a man in late middle life, white-haired, robust, his face vaguely familiar. There was nothing vague about the two younger men. It would have been almost impossible for them to have gone into a street without being recognized.

One was the Minister for Propaganda; the other, his genial-looking Under-Secretary. Both were widely known as radio-speakers and, after the many changes at the Ministry, had proved their capability despite early criticism of their efforts.

The white-haired man's voice was suave and genial.

'I'm glad you have arrived together, Captain Dawlish. I know you by sight, but the others—'

Julia completed the introductions. The white-haired man, it appeared, was Colonel Montgomery.

'And now,' said Montgomery briskly, 'supposing you join us, and we discuss what we have to talk about over dinner?'

'Am I to ask questions, or to receive instructions?' Dawlish inquired mildly.

Arkwright, the Minister of Propaganda, smiled; Fayre, his benevolent assistant, also seemed amused. There was a pause while soup was brought in, and they arranged themselves about the table.

'I will explain a little first,' said Colonel Montgomery. He talked quickly and with the air of a man who knew just what he wanted to say. 'You all know, of course, that this is an unorthodox procedure, and I will tell you at once why you have been summoned here. In short, you have a considerable reputation.'

'I was afraid so,' said Dawlish.

'I hope you won't continue to be afraid,' said Montgomery briskly. 'As a matter of fact your—shall I say adventures?—in the past have given us considerable pleasure. We are going to talk quite freely. Neither Mr. Arkwright nor Mr. Fayre are sticklers for convention, as you will know, and your reputation shows quite clearly that the same can be said of yourself.'

'I think you could say that,' Dawlish murmured.

'Good. And our need at this moment is for two or three men who will be prepared to disregard normal rules and regulations. The matter which we have in hand needs unorthodoxy, and also that quality which the Assistant Commissioner of Scotland Yard calls an "inherent ability to take short-cuts in the furthering of results which the police, hampered as they are by rules and regulations, would take at least three times as long to accomplish". I think I quote him fairly accurately,' added Montgomery dryly.

'Morely's very kind,' murmured Dawlish.

Montgomery's eyes twinkled.

'You haven't always thought so. However, that's neither here nor there. A full dossier of your activities is at the Yard, of course, and after much deliberation we decided to send for you. But before I go on I should make one thing quite clear. There is no obligation on your side to agree to help us.'

'Tell me,' said Dawlish, 'does Morely know you've sent for us?'

'He does not. I hope that only the people in this room know that.'

'Oh,' said Dawlish blankly. 'I see. And then?'

'What do you feel about helping us?' asked Montgomery.

Dawlish rubbed his chin.

'I'm not going to lay down conditions or anything like that, sir, but I would like to know how you contrived to get us away from the camps.'

'In short, who am I?' asked Montgomery. He finished his soup, but before he pressed the bell for service he went on: 'I am a liaison officer between the War Office and the Ministry of Propaganda, Captain Dawlish, with somewhat comprehensive powers. Getting you freed from normal duty was not a matter of great difficulty.'

'Thanks. And if we say "yes" are we acting under orders?'

'That depends on what you call orders. You will be temporarily released from your duties, but you will take instructions from me as far as I am able to give them. Primarily you will work as a free-lance—I do not feel that it would be wise to cramp your powers in any way.'

'It's beginning to sound more than interesting,' said Dawlish, with a certain relish, while the faces of Tim and Ted showed expressions little short of bliss. 'We'll do anything we can, of course. What I did fear was that we might be red-taped.'

'You needn't worry about that,' said Montgomery. He rang for the next course, waiting for an omelette to be served before he spoke again. 'In fact it is precisely because we want to work without any restrictions that we have called on you. We want action, unorthodox action, and quickly.' There was a grim, almost steely note in his voice. 'Let me tell you a little more fully what is troubling us.'

Dawlish and the others listened, giving him all their attention, although during the pauses Dawlish reflected that it was an incredible meeting. The dinner, the courtly friendliness of the three men and Julia Dawnay, the quick, quiet service, was far-removed from anything associated with mystery and subterfuge.

'Briefly, this is the situation,' said Montgomery. 'There is, as you know, a Department of the Ministry of Propaganda which deals with off-setting German and Italian propaganda as well as with spreading ours to neutral countries. That Department is divided into sections, one of which deals primarily with economic business.'

Ted Beresford, who happened to catch his eye at the moment, nodded solemnly.

Montgomery smiled. 'Precisely. Britain delivers the goods. However, in addition to the difficulties of sea transport, the mines and the submarines and, nearer our shores, the air attacks, there is a further matter which is causing us considerable disquiet. The known difficulties can be, and are being, faced, and I think I can say, overcome. But when a difficulty is not known, that is a different matter altogether. And in some neutral countries when goods have been delivered, and are safely in port, they go astray.'

Dawlish stiffened. Tension had sprung into the room. Montgomery, suave and even-voiced, went on speaking.

'The difficulty is not one of normal sabotage; the goods are not destroyed, but misdirected. Agents in the neutral countries—enemy agents, of course—arrange that. It has been particularly noticeable in Eire, and a delay of two or three weeks in delivery of certain manufactured goods frequently throws our plans completely out of gear. Such delays are, of course, additional to those inevitably caused by war-time conditions. You follow me?'

'I couldn't very well miss,' said Dawlish, 'but I'm at a loss. Surely, once the goods reach neutral countries it is up to the authorities there to see that they get to the right destination.'

'That is so. Unfortunately, they do not always succeed.'

'Are you suggesting that we go abroad?' asked Dawlish.

'No, not yet at all events. The trouble starts in England. Someone advises enemy agents what goods are to be misdirected—and generally speaking I think that information goes from the offices of the shipping companies, or of the manufacturers. It is not a question of espionage in a normal way. And it is quite impossible, in view of the state of our relations with several neutral countries, to take any active steps abroad. Our position with Eire, is, of course, extremely delicate. Any attempt on our part to operate there would be open to the gravest suspicion. What are your views on Ireland, Captain Dawlish?'

Dawlish felt the eyes of Fayre and Arkwright on him; and he hesitated before he replied.

'Primarily,' he said, 'I think they distrust us.'

'Ah!' Montgomery was clearly pleased by the answer. 'And secondarily?'

'That they've no need to. I think they should declare for us, of course, although it may be an advantage in some ways to have them neutral. If we had three or four of their naval bases it certainly would be. However, that's probably bias, because I'm English. But as I see it, the de Valera Party, many mistakes though it makes, has one good thing in its favour. It is conscientiously doing its best for Ireland, and it ignores other considerations. I think its policy is wrong, but then,' he added with a smile, 'politics and I never have got on too well together.'

'Generally speaking, then,' said Montgomery, 'you have no prejudice against the Irish Free State?'

'No more than I had against some of our own Governments,' agreed Dawlish.

'Excellent! Personal bias is always a difficult matter to overcome, and the primary thing you have to consider is that there is much genuine goodwill in England for Ireland, and in Ireland for England. We want to consolidate that. You may have heard on the wireless, or read in the evening papers, that a special delegation is in London from Eire at this moment. We know that attempts will be made to sabotage the negotiations. We want to make sure that they will fail. One of the things I want you to do is to try to make sure of that failure, but primarily you will be engaged on finding who is sending the information to Ireland about the goods that go astray.'

Dawlish's thoughts flitted uneasily to Sebastian Bray, imprisoned in 16a, Jermyn Street. He was wondering how to start his story. It would have to be told now, of course: there was no way out of it.

'The main thing, then,' continued Montgomery, 'is this. That organization which is successfully sending information to Eire, and co-operating with an organization in Eire to cause delivery delays, will undoubtedly plan to frustrate our consolidation of goodwill with the Dail. There appears, therefore, to be an opportunity for you to prevent any serious interference with the negotiations, while at the same time finding out who is controlling the operations in this country. If you can do that you will be doing us an inestimable service. Well, Captain Dawlish?'

CHAPTER TEN

HOT RECEPTION

There was silence in the room as all eyes turned towards Dawlish. Dawlish returned Montgomery's level gaze, considered his reply, at some length, and then spoke:

'We shall all three be glad to help where we can, sir.' There was a stiff formality about the words, and Tim and Ted knew that behind them he was thinking quickly. Both men wondered how he would try to slide out of the *impasse* which the arbitrary treatment of Bray had occasioned.

'Good,' said Montgomery, but he also realized that Dawlish was preparing a more pertinent comment, and the silence fell again.

'But before it's finally settled,' went on Dawlish, 'there are some things I would like to know, and some you will want to learn. I'd like to ask my questions first—is that all right?'

'Yes, go on.'

'Why was Miss Dawnay on our train?' demanded Dawlish bluntly.

Montgomery smiled; Julia leaned forward.

'That's easily answered,' said Montgomery. 'She wanted to

make sure that you were not watched on the way from the North.’

‘Was that necessary?’ asked Dawlish.

‘We thought so.’

‘I think it was crazy,’ said Dawlish, and even the Minister of Propaganda sat up sharply in his chair.

‘Indeed?’

‘There you go, you see,’ said Dawlish with complete self-possession. ‘You need the unorthodox, you select me because I am unorthodox and have a habit of doing what I think best and saying what I think. I say some of it, and you freeze me out, or,’ he added with a slow, engaging grin, ‘you try to. You say that you hope only the people in this room know why I’ve been brought south. Yet you send Miss Dawnay to contact me, allowing the possibility of me—and my friends—being brought under suspicion of anyone who is already interested in her activities.’

Montgomery drew a deep breath; it was difficult to be annoyed with Dawlish when he smiled, and despite his words the tone robbed them of offence.

‘It is a possibility,’ Arkwright admitted thoughtfully.

‘I can’t altogether agree,’ said Montgomery. ‘Why should Miss Dawnay be under any kind of suspicion?’

‘I don’t know why,’ said Dawlish. ‘I only know that she was. You have, I suppose, reported the incident at King’s Cross?’ He looked towards her, she nodded.

‘Yes. But there was no one on the train—’

‘Now let’s have this quite straight,’ said Dawlish, pushing his chair back and standing up. ‘You think there was no one on the train, but you can’t be sure. You can’t play at espionage and secret missions and be sure of anything. The operative word is “play”,’ he added, and this time he did not smile. ‘Miss Dawnay’s presence on the train was known, at the station she was deliberately attacked. There is, therefore, a very strong possibility that she was watched throughout the journey. In any case, she was seen at the station with Beresford, Jeremy and me. Another point—you ask "why should Miss Dawnay be under any kind of suspicion"? That wasn't an honest question. You know she is, why try to evade the issue?'

Montgomery pulled at his underlip.

'I think,' said Arkwright quietly, 'that we are satisfied. We have heard much of you, but we wanted to see just how you would react to a certain set of circumstances.'

Dawlish grinned. 'I see your point. Nevertheless, if I'm to tackle this job, I must have your full confidence.'

'You have,' said Montgomery.

'Excellent. I hope you mean that, for it is about to be tested. Do you know Sebastian Bray, Miss Dawnay?'

'No.' Her answer was unhesitating.

'Would you recognize him?'

'I don't think so. I've only seen a newspaper photograph.'

'Right,' said Dawlish briskly. 'You were frightened almost out of your wits on the station, not because of the truck, but because you saw a man who frightened you. A red-haired man. Who is he?'

All eyes were turned towards the girl, and for some seconds she was silent. She had lost a little colour.

'I don't know his name,' she said at last. 'He came to see me a week ago. He warned me not to continue in the special work I'm doing. His manner was a little frightening. When I saw him on the station I'm afraid I lost my head.'

'I can't say that I blame you,' Dawlish acknowledged. 'Did you report the incident?'

'Of course she did,' said Montgomery.

'Was anything done about it?'

'It was disturbing to find that Miss Dawnay's real occupation was known,' said Montgomery, 'and a man from the Special Branch at Scotland Yard was employed, but the red-haired man did not interfere again. After two—no, three—days the guard was taken off Miss Dawnay.'

Dawlish rubbed his chin.

'I don't quite know what to say,' he admitted. 'Miss Dawnay is doing secret work. It is discovered. She has a guard for two days, and then is left alone. There must be some reason for that; the unknown red-head was clearly in a position to get vital facts. His apprehension then, was of utmost importance.'

Montgomery pushed his chair back. Dawlish, by then, was standing by the fireplace, looking down on the six people at the table.

'I have absolute confidence in Miss Dawnay,' Montgomery said, 'and it was her suggestion that she should be unaccompanied—if there were to be other attempts to coerce her they would not be encouraged if she was always watched; she suggested that she would have a better chance of finding the identity of the red-haired man if she was on her own.'

Dawlish eyed Julia speculatively.

'Bait, eh? It was plucky, but apparently not effective. Would you like my honest opinion of your approach to the problem so far?'

'Certainly,' said Arkwright dryly. 'You're probably going to give it anyway.'

Dawlish grinned. 'Well, here it is. A mixture of routine, amateur deduction and the rule of trial and error. Tell me, why isn't the Special Branch engaged? Or for that matter one of the Secret Intelligence departments?'

'So many of their officers are known,' said Montgomery. He was brusque; he had asked for bluntness but did not appear to enjoy it. 'You are not so well known to those people who have—quite clearly—access to the *personnel* of the departments we would normally use. That,' corrected Montgomery swiftly, 'added to the belief that your methods would be more effective.'

'I hope they will be,' said Dawlish grimly. 'If they're not, my advantages are cancelled out; I am known. I was known before Miss Dawnay was seen at King's Cross with me, or I think I was. I—' he hesitated, and his eyes narrowed. 'But was I, by George! Red-head would see us together, add two and two, and come to see me. It explains a lot.' He regarded Montgomery and Julia with a bleak expression. 'I've a nasty feeling that it was a cardinal error.'

Arkwright said softly:

'He came to see *you*?'

'He did. And he told me that I was to be offered off-the-record work. He advised me not to take it, much as he appears to have advised Miss Dawnay.'

'And you reason that it was my fault,' said Julia evenly.

'How else should he guess what was going to be offered me?' asked Dawlish. 'What really made you come on the train?'

Montgomery put in swiftly:

'Miss Dawnay was in the north, and had to travel down today. It appeared a good opportunity for one of us to see you before you were received here, and she took it. If it was an error—'

'It was an error all right,' said Dawlish briskly.

'I'm afraid we shall have to agree,' said Arkwright. 'What happened to the man, Dawlish?'

Dawlish looked at him unsmiling.

'I didn't like his manner, or his chauffeur, who was armed. I thought he would be better under cover for a day or two. With ordinary luck, he won't be on the move just yet.'

Montgomery stared: 'You rendered him *hors de combat*?'

Ted and Tim gulped.

'I think we can say that,' Dawlish said blandly.

'Then where is he?'

'Oh, no,' said Dawlish. 'If I understand the situation properly, I'm detailed to stop this man throwing a spanner into the works of the Eire delegation, and the how of it is up to me. There must be a leakage with you somewhere, you know. If I put his present whereabouts around, it might slip through that leak.'

'That's absurd!' snapped Montgomery. 'Where is he?'

Dawlish put an elbow on the mantel-shelf and said:

'If I tell you, I turn down the proposition, sir. Whether I do or not is entirely up to you.'

'No, that's not necessary,' broke in Arkwright, and he rested a restraining hand on Montgomery's arm. 'Dawlish is quite right, you know. We've promised him *carte blanche*, and before he even knows what he's going to be asked to do, he achieves more than we have done in a month. I think we can safely leave it to you, Dawlish.'

'Thanks,' said Dawlish laconically.

'I—I fully agree,' Montgomery muttered, after a sharp mental struggle.

'Good,' said Dawlish briskly. 'Can Miss Dawnay give me a fuller *precis* of what has been happening?'

'She can,' Montgomery said.

'Good again,' said Dawlish. 'I'd like to brood over this for a short while, and I suggest you all finish your dinner while we go into the foyer. Miss Dawnay can meet us there, and we'll get to my flat to go further into it. Unless you have more definite instructions, sir?'

'Miss Dawnay can do all that is necessary,' said Montgomery.

Chairs were pushed back. Colonel Montgomery moved forward, hand extended.

'We're relying a lot on you Captain Dawlish—and your friends. Good luck.'

'We'll need it,' said Dawlish bluntly.

It was half-an-hour before Julia joined them. They were in the bar, and had already collected Felicity. As Julia swept towards them, a dozen eyes turned to regard her. She was indubitably very lovely, Dawlish decided, and her gown was superb.

Pat introduced her to Felicity.

'I've heard about you,' said Julia, and Dawlish imagined that the two women would get on well. He allowed them little time for talking, however, and within ten minutes of her arrival they were on the way back to Jermyn Street. The Talbot was crowded but not uncomfortably so; through Dawlish's mind passed the hazy reflection that they might have been a party on the way to a night-club in the happier if more wasteful days of peace.

A heavy wind was blowing, and the two women hurried to the porch from the car. Tim stayed to put his own bus and Bray's Alvis away, Dawlish and Beresford accompanied Felicity and Julia to the second floor.

Dawlish opened the front door, and pushed it wide.

As he did so he was met with a wall of smoke. Tongues of flame could be seen licking round the inner door. He drew a deep breath and went forward swiftly, while Beresford grabbed both girls and swung them away.

'There's a stirrup-pump on the landing,' he snapped, 'and extinguishers too, I think. Come on.'

Beresford wrenched two extinguishers from the walls and hurried back, in time to see Dawlish groping his way through an inferno of flame and red-tinged smoke.

In his arms was the body of a man.

CHAPTER ELEVEN

IN THE OPEN

None of the trio looked at Dawlish's burden after the first moment of surprise. They went as near the fire as they could, and began to play the extinguishers. Doors downstairs and upstairs opened, and shadowy figures appeared on the landing.

Dawlish, by the head of the stairs with the man in his arms, saw a tall, thin-faced woman in a dressing-gown hugged tightly about her.

She said brusquely:

'You can take him to my flat.'

Dawlish followed her, thanking the fates for a woman who did not wait to ask unnecessary questions, but who acted with reasonable promptitude. Her flat was on the floor below, and the door was standing open.

'Is he badly hurt?'

'I don't think so.'

He could not speak clearly, for his mouth was thick and dry with smoke and heat. He followed the woman into a room with a bed, and rested his burden on it. The man was small and thin, his clothes scorched and blackened. His long, fair hair was singed in places but the burning was not serious.

Dawlish did not think that he had been overcome by the fumes, nor sufficiently injured by fire to account for his collapse. He stood aside, while a maid brought towel and water, and oddments from the bathroom medical cabinet.

In a detached frame of mind Dawlish watched the older woman's brief examination of the unconscious man, and he was not surprised when, finally, she raised the drooping eyelids.

'May I look?' he said, unaware of the absurdity of making it a request, and he peered into amber-coloured eyes—noting the unusual dilation of the pupils.

The woman let the eyelids fall back.

Her own eyes, grey and tired-looking stared into his.

Dawlish said gravely. 'If I may leave him with you for the time being, I shall be in the flat above, and if you will be so very kind as to ring for Dr. Charles Wintringham, Brook Street, I shall be more than grateful.'

'He hardly needs a doctor,' the woman said.

'I know. But I'd feel happier.' He smiled, turned, and raced up the stairs.

Six people—three wardens, Felicity, Julia and Ted—were milling round the flat. All were marked with signs of the recent fire. Ted was still playing the stirrup-pump, the two women were black with smoke.

'Good work,' said Dawlish. He turned sharply to the wardens. 'I'm having the police here at once, the fire wasn't an accident, I'm afraid.'

'Too much petrol about for *that*, sir,' said the oldest warden.

Dawlish picked up the telephone, and dialled a number, relieved to find it was still working. He asked for the Clarion, room 13, and when the next response came it was Montgomery's voice.

'Dawlish speaking,' said Dawlish. 'I want you to have a word with Scotland Yard, if you will, and ask Inspector Trivett to come here—I think you'll find him in.'

'Is that necessary?' asked Montgomery. 'We don't want your activities to reach the ears of the Yard yet, you know.'

'I don't think we've very much choice,' said Dawlish grimly. 'An attempt has been made to burn me out.'

He put down the receiver a little quicker than was absolutely necessary, and turned to the wardens.

'Well, gentlemen,' he said. 'I'm afraid I'm going to ask the nearly impossible. I want this business kept under your hats. I don't mean the fire,' he added, 'we can't stop talk about that. But it's important that the cause of it isn't generally known. You will have to make your reports, of course, but I think they should be to your Commanding Officer, and in strictest secrecy. Can you manage that?'

The oldest warden smiled.

'We won't make a song about it, sir, if that's what you mean. I'm the Senior Warden on this area, and I know my friends here won't be indiscreet. But I'll have to see the police first, of course.'

'Naturally. Inspector Trivett will be here shortly.'

Dawlish opened a cupboard and produced a couple of bottles of beer. 'There's no reason why you shouldn't have a drink, is there?'

'That's very good of you, sir.'

Before they had been waiting ten minutes Trivett arrived.

It took less than half that time for him to satisfy the wardens and the A.F.S. men, and his own policemen—on guard outside. It appeared that the general belief was that an incendiary bomb had caused the outbreak: that was a satisfactory explanation for general consumption, and Dawlish believed the wardens would be true to their word.

The door closed behind them.

Trivett drew a deep breath, but before he could speak Dawlish took his arm.

'Explanations later, Bill,' he said. 'Have you brought Munk with you?'

'He'll be here in a few minutes.'

'Good. There's someone he can look after. And meanwhile we can take a peek at the gentleman in question. He's not badly hurt.' Leaving a message for Tim to phone the manager in hopes of getting an empty flat for that night, he led Trivett downstairs.

He knew from the Chief Inspector's manner that Montgomery had given him some information, but he did not worry much about that. It was in his mind that Trivett could perhaps identify the man with the amber eyes; he wanted that man identified very badly.

The tall woman in the dressing-gown came forward to meet them.

'I haven't the pleasure of your name,' Dawlish said smilingly, 'but this is Chief Inspector Trivett, of Scotland Yard.'

'How do you do.' The grey head moved slightly. 'My name is Grant—Mrs. Grant.'

'Mrs. Grant has been a great help,' said Dawlish, and he led the way to the room in which he had left the unconscious victim of the fire. The bed was facing the door, and Trivett was able to see the man full-face; Dawlish watched him closely, but saw not the slightest change of expression.

'What *is* this?' demanded Trivett.

Mrs. Grant had retreated so that they were now alone with the man on the bed. Dawlish said slowly:

'I don't know what Montgomery told you, Bill—'

'Practically nothing, except to say that you had authority to act as you thought fit, and that whatever you wanted to talk about was to be in strict confidence.'

'That's something. All right, Bill. That mystery mission I talked to you about earlier was a visit to Montgomery, and it resulted in a commission for a somewhat peculiar job. When we got back the flat was on fire, and this fellow was in my bedroom.'

Trivett said evenly:

'Who put him there?'

'What a lot of suspicion in four words and a look! *I* didn't, Bill. I saw the fire had started by the bedroom, and I couldn't see a reason for the place being fired unless someone was in there. So I went to investigate. I don't know the gentleman from Adam, but I hoped you would.'

'Well, I don't.'

'There's no need to sound so pleased about it,' chided Dawlish. 'He was drugged all right, his pupils are dilated out of recognition. Not a nice thought, is it? A drugged man put in a flat that is set on fire; had I been ten minutes later I doubt if he would be alive now.'

Trivett drew a deep breath.

'I must say you have the devil's own ability to run your head into trouble.'

'This time I've been run into it by someone else,' said Dawlish reproachfully. 'However, it would be a bright idea, I think, to get this chappie's fingerprints, and make sure he's not known at the Yard. Will you do that?' His smile was almost appealing, and Trivett grunted.

'Yes, of course. Munk can look after it. What do you want us to do with him?'

Dawlish chuckled.

'Nicely said! Montgomery's wing is strong, I see, and I am sheltering under it. Do what you like with the chap. A nursing home, perhaps, on the outskirts of the suburbs? I've phoned for a doctor,' he added, 'but I don't think there'll be any danger in moving him.'

'I can do that,' promised Trivett.

'Good man. An idea all ready?'

'Certainly. The Riverside Nursing Home at Staines. I—'

There was a tap on the door, and Dr. Charles Wintringham entered. Broad-shouldered, middle-aged, Dawlish knew him well, and knew also that he occasionally worked with the police, being a pathologist of some renown. He did not waste words but made a quick examination. When that was finished he said briskly:

'Yes, he can be moved—he'll need watching for a day or two. I don't know for sure, but I'd say that he's had a strong dose of one of the morphine groups. You'll arrange for an ambulance, Inspector, won't you?'

'I will,' said Trivett.

Before the ambulance arrived, however, there came Sergeant Munk, Trivett's chief *aide*. A burly man with a fiery moustache and a pair of indignant blue eyes. He nodded to Dawlish, took an impression of the unknown's fingerprints, and was detailed to wait for the ambulance. After thanking Mrs. Grant, Dawlish and Trivett went out.

Except for a uniformed policeman there appeared to be no one in the street, but the darkness made it impossible to be sure.

'I'm not going to try to pretend that I understand it, Bill. I don't. I was hoping I'd get a chance to concentrate on it before any action started, but it looks as if I'm unlucky. Montgomery wasn't enthusiastic about me seeing you, but if you're the personal bodyguard of Sebastian Bray that would be crazy not to get together.'

Trivett peered at him in the darkness.

'Are you on that?'

'On a part of it. I wonder—'

He broke off, for a police ambulance came at speed along the road. Two attendants went into the house, and Dawlish and Trivett waited. It seemed a long time before the men brought the unknown down on a stretcher and, with the help of torches, loaded him into the ambulance. They got in with the patient, while Trivett had a word with the driver.

'Very good, sir,' said the man and revved his engine.

He started off quickly, but he did not go far. There was a violent grinding of brakes, and Dawlish and Trivett, about to enter the house, swung round.

They could just see the dark shape of the ambulance before it crashed.

The crash echoed up and down Jermyn Street, growing worse as the ambulance, right out of control, heeled over on its side.

Trivett and Dawlish started to run towards it.

But before they were half-way there Dawlish gripped the Inspector's arm, and snapped:

'Get down, Bill!'

Instinctively Trivett obeyed; duty that often took him out by night had taught him the need for split-second action, and without knowing the reason for such an order he flung himself face-downwards; Dawlish did the same, but kept his eye on a swift-moving shadow of an on-coming motor-cycle driver without lights.

And then there was a sharp thud near the ambulance, a blinding flash, and an explosion which lifted both men bodily and hurled them against the nearest house.

CHAPTER TWELVE

DAWLISH HAS DOUBTS

Slowly Dawlish rose to his feet.

Perhaps the most astonishing thing for some seconds was the utter silence which followed the explosion. The windows were smashed in nearby houses, but no lights showed—it might have been a street of the dead. There was no doubt that everyone within them believed it to be a bomb, and kept wisely out of danger. Presently he saw the dipped headlights of a car coming towards him, and a moment later a warden flashing his torch not a yard away from him. Temporarily deafened by the explosion Dawlish pointed to his ears, and approached the wreckage.

By this time Trivett was also on his feet gesturing to the warden.

The debris of the ambulance was appalling.

Not only had that been blown to pieces, but the three men inside it were gone. By some freak of the explosion the driver had been flung from his seat, landing, unconscious but not seriously hurt, against the kerb.

The wardens, thick as flies by then, were already busy

searching the wreckage. Dawlish and Trivett waited only until the body of the yellow-haired man was brought out. That he was dead, there was no doubt.

Dawlish feeling sick, turned back to the flat.

His hearing was now well enough for him to catch Trivett's gloomy comment:

'Well, Pat! They came in the open that time.'

'And told us something,' said Dawlish, his voice appearing to come from a long way off. 'The unholy swine! There's death and disaster enough without this. I—' he stopped, and then went on: 'Well, I suppose that kind of talk isn't going to get us anywhere.' He regarded Trivett curiously. 'You take it calmly, old man.'

Trivett shrugged.

'There's been so much violence, Pat. It's part of life. It isn't the less ghastly for all that, but one learns to stand it. What did you mean when you said "they'd told us something"?'

'They wanted the long-haired chap dead,' said Dawlish.

'They'd made that fairly obvious before,' said Trivett.

'Had they? I'm not sure. In the flat he might have been merely a body put there to incriminate me. In the ambulance he was attacked because he himself had to die. In short, he might have been dangerous alive. That's obvious, isn't it?'

Trivett said cautiously: 'It's no use jumping to conclusions.'

'Jumping to conclusions my hat,' said Dawlish sharply. 'The facts shout at you. However, by a process of diversions you'll reach the same conclusion this time tomorrow, Bill.' He grinned. 'I'm working on the assumption that they wanted the chap dead. That there's a connection with Bray I don't doubt. Once we find it we might be half-way to a solution.' He stopped outside the closed front door of the flat. 'Odd that Ted didn't come out to see what was what,' he said. He rang the bell sharply, and went on:

'I think we'll have to get Montgomery to agree to you knowing precisely what I'm doing, Bill. Working at cross purposes won't help us.'

Trivett shrugged.

'Montgomery isn't the easiest of men to handle.'

Dawlish frowned. 'He gave me that impression too. Stiff with regulations but going through the painful process of trying not to be.' He pressed the bell again, more insistently. 'I feel as if I've been dropped into the middle of a Walt Disney Symphony,' he admitted, 'but some things are taking shape. I—come on, folk, we don't want to stay here all night.'

He rang the bell again, but there was no answer.

Then for the first time he looked in some alarm at Trivett. Trivett said quietly:

'Perhaps they've gone to another flat—you told them to find one, didn't you?'

'They wouldn't go without waiting for me,' said Dawlish sharply. 'Stand back a bit.' He drew away from the door himself, and launched himself at it. Trivett had previously seen his remarkable strength exerted, but was startled by the force of the assault.

A second lunge was enough to break it open, and Dawlish staggered through. Trivett was on his heels, and they saw exactly the same thing; an empty room.

Dawlish did not speak, but stepped swiftly to the bedroom, the door of which was standing open; that too was empty. In thirty seconds they had looked in every room of the flat, to find no sign of Ted or the two women. Dawlish, by then, was tight-lipped and pale. There was a bleakness about him which impressed Trivett. He stepped to the telephone and lifted it.

'Has there been a call from here lately?' he asked the operator of the flats, to be told:

'Not for twenty minutes or more, sir.'

'Who was the last one to, do you know?'

'The Clarion Hotel, sir—we have a system which tells us the number called although the dialling can be direct. I—'

'That's all right,' said Trivett abruptly.

Until then he had believed that there was a simple enough explanation; now he felt as bleak as Dawlish looked. The large man had gone into the kitchen and was opening the door which led to the fire-escape. He shone a torch about the iron landing, and the beam fell on a small square of white. Trivett saw him stoop and retrieve a handkerchief.

As Dawlish came back, there was a sound of approaching footsteps. Tim Jeremy's long face appeared round the door, a picture of stupefaction. 'What the hell . . .'

'Have you seen Ted and the others?' snapped Dawlish.

'T-T-Ted? No, I've been putting the cars away.' He looked about the fire-charred rooms, and then at the gaunt face of his friend.

'They were here fifteen minutes ago,' snapped Dawlish. 'The only way they could have gone out without being noticed was by the back door.' He was silent for a moment, and then he slowly raised his right hand. In it was the handkerchief. It smelt faintly of violets. 'This is Felicity's. And she wouldn't go out of the back way for the sake of it—nor would the others for that matter. Bill, get some men busy making inquiries, will you?'

Trivett turned decisively.

'I'll do what I can,' he said.

'There isn't going to be much chance of results on a night as black as this,' said Tim Jeremy. 'Pat, they can't have been spirited away. And what *has* happened?'

Dawlish said tersely:

'I fancy it's a hostage for a hostage; or, more accurately, three prisoners for two.'

'Don't be an idiot! Ted wouldn't let himself be taken out without kicking up a shindy.'

'Who said there wasn't a shindy?' demanded Dawlish. 'We'll try the other flats, Tim. You go upstairs.'

Mrs. Grant, long-suffering, still in her dressing-gown, could not help him; she had been awakened by the explosion, but when she had heard no planes overhead she had dozed off again. She was sorry, but—

Dawlish apologized for disturbing her, and tried the ground floor flat; no one had heard anything there. He returned to the second floor flat, to find Tim just arrived from upstairs.

'Not a sound nor a sign except the explosion,' he said.

'The same with me.' Dawlish lit a cigarette, and drew at it sharply. 'I don't like it, Tim. I don't like any of this blasted business. I doubt whether we've been given a straight story.'

'What *do* you mean?'

'Julia Dawnay. If she doesn't shout suspicion I'd like to know who does. Damn it, everything she's done has been phoney from the start.'

Tim sniffed. 'Aren't you being a bit well . . .'

His words were so full of feeling that momentarily Dawlish was startled. Tim was staring at him with more than a touch of hostility.

Dawlish's voice had an oddly casual sound.

'Why not, Tim? The argument's sound.'

'I don't think so,' asserted Timothy doggedly. 'Montgomery might have been phoney had he been on his own, but getting us out of camp argues against it. Arkwright and Fayre certainly aren't up to any tricks. They've vouched for Julia. That's good enough for me, old man.' His voice had a note of finality which was rare, for in most things Tim Jeremy was prepared to take Dawlish's word without question.

Dawlish pushed a hand through his hair.

'So it's that way, Tim.'

No touch of humour or compromise crossed Tim's face.

'Until you took a dig at her I didn't think of it. But I'll stake all I've got on Julia.'

Dawlish nodded amicably; but his doubts of Julia remained. She *could* have contrived to persuade the others to leave the flat, even if at the point of a gun. But he could not enlarge on this possibility or air his suspicions to Tim; Tim had fallen for Julia Dawnay, and in a different moment Dawlish would have felt a sympathetic understanding. But now he was afraid for Felicity and for Ted. It was not good to be afraid.

There was a brief flurry of activity in the next ten minutes. Det. Sergeant Munk, who had been to the Yard, returned: there was no record of the unknown's fingerprints in Records Department. Trivett also returned; wardens and police had noticed nothing. All had pointed out that at the time of the explosion they had left their usual posts to hurry into Jermyn Street. The night-manager arrived, to inquire into the effects of the fire. He was suave, helpful, not outwardly perturbed. Yes, he could find another flat for Mr. Jeremy; he made no mention of 16a, to Dawlish's relief.

He left the flat, while Dawlish, Trivett and Jeremy looked helplessly at each other; even Dawlish had been knocked off his balance by the sudden rush of events. There was silence for some seconds, and then as Trivett opened his mouth, the telephone rang.

It startled them all.

Dawlish stepped quickly towards it and lifted the receiver.

'Captain Jeremy's flat.'

'Let me speak to Captain Dawlish, please,' said a mellow voice civilly enough; but to Dawlish there was something frightening in it, frightening because the voice was undoubtedly that of the man who had called himself Sebastian Bray.

CHAPTER THIRTEEN

SECOND MEETING

For a moment Dawlish was too startled to think; then, as his mind began to move more freely, he motioned to Trivett with his free hand. Trivett nodded briefly and hurried from the flat to seek another telephone where with luck he could get the source of the call established.

'Dawlish speaking.'

There was a pause, before Bray said softly:

'So, Captain Dawlish, you are still alive. How very fortunate for you.'

'But not quite so fortunate for you,' said Dawlish sharply.

'Do you think so? I told you in your flat that I could handle any emergency; you should have taken me at my word.'

'A very rash thing to do, and one I would certainly not recommend,' said Dawlish evenly. 'What do you want?'

'A talk with you,' said Bray. 'And lest you should think it wise to broadcast the news of the meeting, I shall remind you of my remarks about Miss Deverall, and the unfortunate liability to accidents in these turbulent days. You understand me, I hope?'

'Oh, yes, I understand you,' said Dawlish. 'Where?'

'It will not be quite as easy as that,' said Bray. He laughed; it was not a pleasant sound. 'I shall meet you, or send an emissary for you, at the corner of Haymarket and Coventry Street. In precisely half-an-hour, Captain Dawlish. If you are wise you will come alone, and follow my messenger without question.'

Dawlish replaced the receiver slowly, and kept his hand on it while he looked at Tim. Tim appeared to be a long way off, and, what was more, he seemed to be a stranger, someone who had nothing to do with what was happening in the flat, or what had been said over the telephone. There was a heavy weight of depression in Dawlish's breast, something he had known before when there had been danger for Felicity, but which he had hoped he would never experience again.

Tim said: 'What is it, Pat?'

'The expected threat,' said Dawlish curtly. 'It runs truer to form than any Derby favourite.' There was a savage note in his voice, a savage expression in his eyes. 'Tim, I'm meeting a man Bray is sending, and I'm going alone—before Trivett gets back. It's half-past ten now. If I have not returned by two o'clock, get in touch with Montgomery or one of the others, and tell them everything.'

Tim said slowly: 'Why go alone?'

'For once I'm going to do what I'm told,' said Dawlish. 'It's no use arguing, old man, and, after all, I hope to locate Julia as well as Felicity and Ted.' He forced a smile. 'When Trivett gets back, tell him I've been called away by Montgomery.'

Jeremy's inclination was to follow him without saying what he proposed to do. But in his long association with Dawlish he had learnt to trust his judgment.

He shrugged, and said briefly:

'Good hunting, old man.'

'I'll make it good,' said Dawlish.

He went briskly out of the room, while Jeremy alone and in a melancholy mood, sought for, and found, a bottle of beer. He was drinking it when Trivett returned.

'Where's Dawlish?' demanded Trivett promptly.

'Montgomery called him,' lied Tim as quickly.

'Where are they meeting?'

'I haven't a notion,' said Tim. 'Pat can be as close as an oyster when he likes, and he's not in a talkative mood just now, anyhow. Did you have any luck?'

Trivett said quietly:

'I don't know, but I traced that call. It came from the Clarion Hotel, but it was from one of the public call-boxes there. I'm going over there—are you coming?'

'I think yes,' said Jeremy, and there was relief in his mind at the thought that he had something to do. He found it odd to have his thoughts divided between Dawlish and Julia; he was finding his feelings for Julia mixed and troubled. He did not believe Dawlish's suspicions of her to be justified; but he could not forget them.

Twice the wind made Dawlish catch his breath as he hurried towards the far end of Jermyn Street. Clouds obscured the stars and a few splashes of rain touched his face as he turned into the doorway of 16a, and let himself into the ground-floor flat.

The small room where he had left Bray was empty, and the fantastic thought that there could be a man who looked like Sebastian Bray and also talked like him disappeared. He was glad. The confusion was already bad enough. He looked at the keyhole of the locked door, and he saw the faint scratches made by a skeleton key.

He did not waste time in blame or vain regret. He had hoped his visit to Number 16a earlier in the evening had been unobserved; he was wrong, and the consequences of his error might be even further-reaching than the immediate result.

At that moment it was difficult for him to see beyond the personal angle. There was, in fact, an argument in his mind: should he go to the rendezvous as instructed, in an attempt to find out where Felicity and Ted were, or was his right course to tell Montgomery or Trivett?

He settled the argument as he walked slowly towards Piccadilly.

He had been told to use his own judgment, and his judgment assured him that the man he knew as Sebastian Bray was a fraud—whether Trivett thought so or not did not matter. If the man was an impersonator, then it was probable that he was at least acquainted with the organization which was causing difficulty in neutral countries, particularly in Eire. The job, he, Dawlish, had been given to do was to find the main organizer: to take Tim or the police to the meeting place would probably preclude all possibility of a talk with Bray, and that would mean stalemate all round.

But *was* it Bray?

Dawlish had not settled that question when he reached Piccadilly. He had fifteen minutes left of the half-an-hour at his disposal. On an impulse he hailed a passing cabby. The man pulled up, and Dawlish handed him a ten-shilling note.

'Go to the nearest newspaper office,' he said, 'and get me a copy of a photograph of Mr. Sebastian Bray—have you got that name?'

'Okay sir, yes.'

'Bring it to the corner of Haymarket—the Leicester Square side,' said Dawlish, 'and make it the fastest black-out run you've done. All right?'

'Okay, sir.'

Dawlish walked slowly towards the rendezvous. He had by now precisely five minutes to spare.

And then, very suddenly, a car drew up beside him. A voice called him from the driving-seat.

'Mr. Dawlish, please.'

Dawlish stepped forward. There was not enough light for him to see clearly, but enough to recognize the swarthy-faced chauffeur.

'Before I get in,' said Dawlish chattily, 'perhaps it would be as well to tell you that I have a gun.'

'I don't care if you've twenty.'

'That might be a little over-doing it,' answered Dawlish, whose spirits, at the thought of danger ahead were soaring, 'both as to the quantity of guns and your alleged state of mind.'

'Get *in*,' said the chauffeur, 'and now listen to me. If you think you can get us followed—'

Dawlish restrained a strong temptation to punch the man on the nose; it was a sharp, unpleasant nose, and overlong. 'Oh, by the way, I've sent a cabby to get me some cigarettes. He'll be here in a moment.'

'He'd better be.'

The 'moment' drew out to seven minutes, and the chauffeur grew impatient; but he did not drive off alone, which told Dawlish that Bray's instructions had been precise. Dawlish rewarded the cabby with a pound on top of the first ten shillings, took the photograph, and climbed into the big car.

The chauffeur let in the clutch immediately.

Dawlish sat back in the dark interior; relieved to find there was no one else inside. Casually he lit a cigarette, shading the flame with his hands, and then he slipped the photograph from the envelope, and looked at it by the light of a cupped pencil torch.

For a second time he was disappointed. For there was no doubt that the photograph of Sebastian Bray was of the man he had seen at King's Cross, and met later at the flat. All chance that Bray was being impersonated faded.

Dawlish closed his eyes and sat back.

It was useless to try to find where he was going; he could rely only on the time the journey took. It was fifteen minutes later by his watch, when the car stopped.

Dawlish half-expected to find that he had been brought by a roundabout route to the Clarion Hotel, but that hope did not materialize. He climbed down outside one of a series of large houses in a residential part of London which he could not hope to identify.

Dawlish followed the chauffeur to what he soon realized to be a cellar which had been turned into an air-raid shelter.

Sebastian Bray stood on the threshold, and beyond him Dawlish saw Ted, Felicity and Julia, and a man whose face was half-hidden by the handkerchief which gagged him, but whom Dawlish recognized with a shock which momentarily sickened him.

Colonel Montgomery was a prisoner in that house.

CHAPTER FOURTEEN

BRAY IS CONFIDENT

Dawlish's expression did not alter, even when he saw the quick horror in Felicity's eyes, an expression which pulled at his heart. He looked about the underground room, and then again at Felicity. It was as if he had no fear in the world, as if he had come to see her at the flat, and no one else was there. He stepped towards her, putting his arms about her shoulders.

'Hallo, darling! I wasn't too long, I hope?'

'Oh, Pat!' There was despair in her voice, and her arms tightened about him, and yet he knew that for a moment her heart had lifted. He attempted to take her with him to the side of the large cellar and two vacant chairs, but after two steps she stopped.

The silence of the others was a queer thing. All attention was riveted on Dawlish.

He glanced down, and saw that Felicity had a rope tied about her ankle, and fastened to an iron ring in the wall. He turned about slowly, slipping his right hand into his pocket. Bray said sharply:

'Take your hand away, Dawlish!'

In the man's voice was a hint of panic, as if he realized for the first time that in Dawlish there was something incalculable. Dawlish took his hand from his pocket, but not hurriedly. In it he held a small knife. With precision, but no noticeable haste, he opened the blade and bent to the rope.

'Don't cut that!' snapped Bray.

'Drop that knife!' snarled the chauffeur.

Dawlish, holding the rope firmly in his left hand, cut through it. The knife, although sharp, took some seconds to sever the thick strands, and in that time the chauffeur took three steps forward, his gun aimed at Dawlish's head. Julia drew a deep breath. Felicity stood quite still.

Dawlish finished his job, and stood up, moving with Felicity to the vacant chairs.

Bray cleared his throat. It was obvious that he was in two minds as to his next move; then he allowed his gaze to rest speculatively on Felicity.

It was odd, thought Dawlish, that from the first he had tried to attack him through her; there was some reason for that, or the man would not have made such a point of it.

'What do you think I brought the girl here for?'

'I don't know,' said Dawlish, 'but I do know that it was another of your mistakes, Bray. You quite litter London with them, don't you? If you'd kept her here and talked to me somewhere else, you might have had some luck, but, speaking personally, I hardly think so.'

'Why, you fool, I'm armed—'

'I have a fist,' said Dawlish mildly.

It was absurd, of course; there was no reason for his confidence, and he knew that as well as the others present. Nevertheless, a stranger looking into the room might have thought that it was Dawlish, not Bray, who held the trump cards. Ted Beresford had seen similar displays before, as had Felicity; to Julia, Bray and the chauffeur—as well as to Colonel Montgomery—it was something quite new, and for the first time they were able to assess Dawlish from personal experience; his behaviour was far, far in excess of what they had been led to expect from his reputation. His calm and his confidence were alike uncanny.

His eyes met Bray's, and Bray's dropped. Dawlish went on in a mild voice:

'On the telephone you said you wanted to talk.'

Bray drew in a sharp breath.

'My dear Dawlish, the main point of that telephone call was to get you here, and that is accomplished.' The words seemed to give Bray a greater confidence. He drew nearer to Dawlish, although he did not come too close; it was as if he feared the big man's fist in spite of the automatic in his chauffeur's hand. 'I've got all of you now, and that's just what I wanted. I tried to warn you—I don't kill people for the sake of it, *but*'—his voice took on a softer, menacing note—'I don't let *anyone* stand in my way.'

'Surprise, surprise,' murmured Dawlish. 'Where have I heard those grandiloquent words before?'

'I'm not easy to bluff,' said Bray, his voice rising a little. 'I had you watched, and had a report telephoned—you weren't followed, no one knows where you are.' He eyed Dawlish keenly. 'Well, what are you going to do about it?'

'I'm waiting to hear your proposition first,' said Dawlish.

Bray laughed, and the sound was not pleasant.

'That's easy. I'm negotiating with your precious politicians tomorrow. To make it doubly safe I've brought you all here just to make sure you can't do any harm. Got me?'

'Not yet,' said Dawlish.

'You want it spelt out?'

'Oh, no. I gather your drift,' said Dawlish, 'but I haven't got you—yet. It's as well to remember the old adage: He laughs best who laughs last.' Dawlish stifled a yawn. 'Sorry, it's getting late. Where do we sleep?'

'You don't,' snapped Bray.

'No? What do we do?'

Bray drew a deep breath.

'You're thicker-witted than I thought you were! You've come here to die, Dawlish; don't make any mistake about that. You see, Dawlish'—there was a low, savage note in his voice as he went on—'you and Dawnay and perhaps Montgomery had ideas about one thing. You thought I might not be the real Bray. And if I was the real Bray, you thought I was up to something that wasn't put in the dispatches between London and Dublin. You were right on one count—guess which one.'

Dawlish said flippantly: 'Oh, you're Bray all right.'

'So you'll grant me that. All right, I'm Bray. Work that out in the little time you've got left.'

'You're still suffering under a delusion,' said Dawlish. 'I didn't come here to fade out, Bray; I came to get your hostages.'

'Ses you.'

'Crude, but certainly applicable,' said Dawlish lightly. He stretched his legs out to a more comfortable position.

'I'll get what I want from you,' snapped Bray. 'How long have you been working against me, Dawlish?'

The question startled Dawlish, although in some measure it satisfied him; Bray *did* want something. What foul schemes there had been in his mind to make him talk Dawlish did not know; that Felicity and the rope played some part in it he had seen from the first, and he had acted on that belief. But he had not expected to find that Bray believed he had been working for some time.

There was no need to reassure the gentleman.

Gently Dawlish shook his head.

'No can talk,' he said, and he actually looked across at Ted Beresford and grinned. 'No want to talk,' he added. 'Bray, I'm giving you ten minutes to free everyone here and to let them go.'

'Why, you damned fool—'

'Let me have a crack at him,' implored the chauffeur, but Bray snapped:

'Leave this to me, Pell. You aren't leaving here, Dawlish. But if you tell me the truth I'll make it quick for the lot of you.'

'It surprises me that you don't see what's staring you in the face, Bray,' said Dawlish conversationally. 'Do I strike you as a man scared out of his wits, or one about to die? I do not?—excellent. There's the evidence. Take it from me, that if you don't use the ten minutes grace I've given you you'll be the sorriest man in London.'

Bray stared; Pell licked his lips. Both men could not evade the confidence of Dawlish's manner, both were wondering if there could be anything in what he said; and Dawlish wanted to create just such an attitude in their minds.

'Perhaps you're too excited to think things out clearly, so I'll explain them to you,' Dawlish went on. 'You want us dead; right, we'll grant that point. But you also want this house. It's a very comfortable house, I imagine, and the cellar has been reinforced with considerable care, which shows a certain regard for your own skin. The indication, then, is that you're fond of your own life, and intend to keep it. So, I'm offering you a bargain—your life for ours.'

Bray's eyes glared at Beresford as the latter said Casually:

'How are you working it?'

'Fairly simply,' said Dawlish. 'I brought a tube of nitroglycerine with me. Nasty stuff, nitro. A small tube—half the size of a fountain-pen—would blow this cellar and most of this house to pieces, Sebastian Bray and all. Not a nice thought. But we can afford it—if we've got to die, we can take him with us. If he wants to live, he's got to let us go. The nitro is delicate stuff to handle, Bray will know that, and any attempt at rough stuff on me will send up the whole works. Checkmate, Bray—or don't you think so?'

He stared at the man, his eyes cold.

CHAPTER FIFTEEN

IS IT BLUFF?

There was utter silence in the cellar for an appreciable time. Dawlish had spoken with such certainty that Bray almost believed him.

At last Bray snapped:

'You're lying, Dawlish. I'm not going to fall for an old trick like that.'

Dawlish said wearily: 'Do try to use a little common sense, Bray. I know you'd stop at nothing—the affair with the ambulance proves that. I know also that you're playing for high stakes, and that you think I might be able to put a spoke in your wheel. And Montgomery might, for that matter. Do you think I'd come here, knowing all that, without taking some precautions? Being followed was useless—I needed something which would be decisive for the time being at least—and I found it. Actually I lifted the idea out of a book,' he added amiably. 'It worked all right there.'

'This isn't a book!' snapped Bray.

'No-o,' admitted Dawlish, 'but the description of the ensuing explosion was really well done. Much debris and disaster. I was so interested that I checked up the effects of nitro-glycerine with an explosives expert. It does all that is claimed for it, and more. You'll notice that I've moved very slowly while I've been here. I don't want to upset the apple-cart, you know.'

Julia Dawnay said in a strangled voice:

'Do you mean you're carrying enough explosive in your pocket to blow us sky-high?'

'Precisely,' said Dawlish.

'The smart alec's lying!' snarled Pell. 'Let me have a crack at him, Guv'nor!'

Bray did not answer, did not move his gaze from Dawlish's. The large man returned his stare equably. It was checkmate; Dawlish knew it as he watched the man's expression change, and he knew more than that.

Bray wanted him and—presumably the others—dead.

With a little ingenuity he could leave the cellar at small risk to himself, leaving his prisoners to die. Bray did not try that, *therefore Bray could not afford to let the house be destroyed.*

Clearly that meant that it was the headquarters of whatever organization he was controlling, or helping to control.

Dawlish leaned back, half-closing his eyes.

'I'm very patient, Bray.'

'I—don't—believe—you've—got—anything,' said Bray very softly. Then more quickly. 'I don't believe any man would have the nerve.'

'No?' said Dawlish.

He sprang to his feet, so quickly that Felicity jumped, and Bray backed sharply away. Pell uttered a short exclamation, and his face paled. Dawlish thrust his right hand to his pocket.

'All right, damn you, we'll get it over!'

'Stop, Dawlish! Stop!'

There was a film of sweat on the man's forehead, and his

cheeks were ashen. Dawlish kept still, his hand still at his pocket.

'Well?' said Dawlish.

'I—I'll make it worth your while to keep out of this,' said Bray after a pause which seemed to have lasted for a long time. 'I'll make it ten thousand pounds, Dawlish. You and Beresford and your girl can go. Get out, let me carry on for the next three days, and it will be worth ten thousand pounds to you.' Desperately afraid, the man stared into Dawlish's eyes.

And Dawlish laughed.

'Oh, no,' he said. 'It's your finish, Bray. You'll have a chance to get away with your life, but nothing else. A big mistake, you see. I've told you all along that you were making mistakes—wasn't it you who advised me to believe what I was told? Hoist with your own petard, don't they say?' He took his hand sharply from his pocket, and the electric lamp glinted on glass.

And he tossed the glass towards Pell and Bray!

Both men screamed.

Both men cowered back, Pell dropping his hands, Bray covering his face in sudden terror. The glass struck Pell's shoulder, but while it was breaking, Dawlish leapt forward and wrenched his gun away.

He turned on Bray.

In the split-second that all of them had been waiting for the explosion—even Felicity's cheeks had lost their colour, she, too, had found it hard to believe that Dawlish had been bluffing—it seemed that a dozen things happened at once. Dawlish swung his left fist to Bray's stomach, following it up with a crashing blow—the second time in five hours that such a blow had been delivered to the envoy from Eire, and with the same effect as the first. Pell had staggered to the door, but he was a quick-thinking rogue, and he had realized that the nitro-glycerine talk had been bluff. He jumped at Dawlish, trying to regain his gun.

Dawlish let him run into a straight left.

It brought Pell up sharply. Dawlish struck him on the jaw with the butt of the automatic, and Pell slithered backwards, as unconscious as his employer.

Ted called:

'Grand work, Pat!'

No one else spoke, while Dawlish turned to see Felicity's eyes shining into his. He grinned at her, took his knife from his pocket and handed it over. 'Get Julia unfastened,' he said. 'We may not have a lot of time.'

In something under sixty seconds Julia and Beresford were free, and the gag had been taken from Montgomery's mouth. Dawlish cut the cord at the Colonel's wrists and ankles, but when Montgomery tried to stand his legs gave way beneath him.

'Five minutes massage will put you right,' Dawlish said. 'We'll get you upstairs first. How many others have you seen on the premises, Ted?'

'Two. Both roughnecks.'

'Get Bray's gun and take the head of these stairs,' said Dawlish. He put the gun he had taken from Pell into Felicity's hand, motioned her and Julia to follow Beresford, then lifted Montgomery in his arms and carried him effortlessly in the wake of the girls. There was no sign of trouble in the hall, and Ted's figure was no more than a shadow against the head of the stairs.

Dawlish reached the car outside a yard or two behind Felicity, who had slipped into the driving-seat. As he lowered Montgomery into the tonneau, the Colonel opened his mouth for the first time.

'I—I shall never be able to thank you, Dawlish.'

'It's early to say that,' smiled Dawlish. 'I'm going to get Bray. I hope,' he added.

'Hurry,' said Felicity in a subdued voice.

He nodded at her although in the darkness he could not see her face, and hurried back to the front door. As he reached it he heard a nasal voice say clearly:

'What the hell!'

Beresford's voice followed, low but insistent.

'Keep right where you are!' There was a moment of silence, and then the sharp report of a revolver shot. Another followed. Keeping close to the wall Dawlish saw Ted backing towards him, and at the head of the staircase a man's hand holding a gun.

Dawlish fired.

He scored a hit, for a muttered curse came as the hand was sharply withdrawn. But it was not the finish. There were others both upstairs and down. Footsteps were echoing, voices were whispering. Beresford took a shot at a man behind the lower door, but it did no more than bury itself in the wall nearby. A shot flashed between Dawlish and Beresford, smashing through the glass panel of the front door. Dawlish prayed that it did not touch anyone in the car outside.

Beresford backed more swiftly.

As he reached the front door a volley of shots rang out from the head of the stairs.

Dawlish and Beresford reached the porch.

Dawlish said urgently:

'Try and find the back way, Ted.'

But they were doomed to interruption. The shooting had stopped, but heavy footsteps pounded along the road, and two torches showed, behind them a warden and a policeman. The policeman put a whistle to his lips, and the summons shrilled up and down the street.

'Stay where you are!' he ordered as Dawlish moved.

Desperately, Dawlish spoke.

'Constable, there are a dozen dangerous men in that house— they mustn't get out. Do you know the back exit?'

The man hesitated.

'I'll come with you,' snapped Beresford. 'We're not trying to get away.'

But seconds were passing. Other men came as if spirited from the shadows, and in less than two minutes four, including Beresford, were going to the back of the house. As they hurried, however, Dawlish heard the sound of a car engine.

A second, and a third followed.

There was a sudden flash of flame from the house, and as it came both men flung themselves down, just as Dawlish and Trivett had done earlier in the evening. There was no time for Dawlish to try to help Felicity.

The explosion came then.

It echoed and reverberated about the street, and yet it was not so violent as Dawlish had expected it to be. There was a crashing of bricks and mortar, glass and debris blew out and in.

Dawlish straightened up, without any injury. The policeman staggered to his feet, holding his right hand against his cheek.

Dawlish said urgently:

'Are you fit enough to get the firemen here?'

'Y-yes, sir.' The man turned and began to hurry along the road, while the fire inside the house grew fiercer and brighter. Dawlish thanked the fates that it was a raid-free night as he looked round, saw that Felicity and Julia were all right, and then stepped towards the front door, which was hanging drunkenly open. The flames could just be seen, fiercer by far than anything which there had been at Jermyn Street, and Dawlish's figure stood, a clear silhouette, against them as he entered the hall.

Felicity's voice echoed after him.

'Pat, don't go!'

But Dawlish went on.

CHAPTER SIXTEEN

DIPLOMATIC INTERLUDE

There was nothing he could do.

The explosion had occurred in the cellar. He had no doubt at all that it had been done deliberately, and because it was known by whoever had left the house last that the contents of the cellar must not fall into the hands of the authorities. Dawlish reached the top of the cellar stairs, but it was useless to attempt to go down into the inferno below.

He turned, almost cannoning into Felicity.

'Hallo, my sweet,' he said, and he flung his arm about her 'Isn't it bad enough for one of us to play the fool?' In the glow of the fire she could see that he was smiling at her, although the red reflection and the shadows cast by flickering flames showed his face in an almost sinister light.

They went silently out of the house.

Except through the front door, which could not be closed, the fire was not visible outside. Dawlish leaned against the side of the car. He felt suddenly tired and exhausted. The feeling of fatigue grew overpowering. He closed his eyes, and Felicity looked at him anxiously.

Footsteps came from the by-road.

Beresford and two of the policemen who had gone with him returned. They had had no luck, of course—arriving just in time to see the rear light of one of the cars disappearing.

Dawlish stifled a yawn.

'They didn't lose much time,' he said.

'They must have been waiting for it,' opined Beresford.

'More or less. I wonder if Bray and Pell got away?'

'Not likely,' said Beresford, 'and I can't say that I'm sorry. The end of a nasty affair.'

Dawlish, sombre in the red glow, stared. His eyes looked as if they were on fire, and the glow gleamed on his teeth as he spoke.

'I don't think so, Ted. A chapter, that's all. It's just beginning.'

With exemplary patience the policeman—a sergeant—had stood by listening. Now he cleared his throat.

'I think it's time you told me more about it, sir.'

Dawlish turned his head.

'And rightly, sergeant. If it will set your mind at rest, I'm working with Chief Inspector Trivett—'

'*Are* you, sir?' The man looked startled.

'And he'll confirm that,' said Dawlish. 'Will you get in touch with him at the Yard? The quicker we can get away the better.'

The sergeant considered.

'As soon as the fire-brigade's here I'll come to a telephone with you,' he said, and five minutes later he was as good as his word. Trivett was not at the Yard, but Det. Sergeant Munk was there, and he told the sergeant sufficient for the man to regard Dawlish with respect.

'That's all right, sir. If you will report to the Inspector—you can't tell me what happened, can you?'

'I don't know very much,' said Dawlish, and again he stifled a yawn. 'And another thing. The cellar is completely gutted by now. I think there might be two men there,' he went on quickly: 'I went in, but there wasn't a chance of getting below stairs. But look for them, sergeant.'

'I certainly will, sir.'

'And I'll give you my card,' said Dawlish.

He did so, and then stepped into the car. He did not think there was a great chance of Bray or Pell escaping, and that meant that he would have much more trouble in finding out who had helped in the directing of operations.

Someone had.

Someone in that house had been in a position to cause the explosion, and that meant a man with considerable authority—and one who could act very swiftly in emergency. From the time the shooting had started to the time that the house had been blown up, no more than ten minutes had passed.

Felicity was already getting into the driving-seat again, and the car drove off. Vaguely it passed through Dawlish's mind that the car itself provided something in the nature of a clue; it might be traced back to Bray, or to someone else. He hoped it would be someone else. He wished that he was not so tired, but his head nodded, his chin drooped to his chest, and he was sleeping. Felicity had learned from the sergeant that they were in St. John's Wood, and in fifteen minutes she turned into Jermyn Street.

There Dawlish awakened with a start.

Ted had been rubbing Montgomery's ankles, and the Colonel was able to step from the car on his own volition. He had been very silent, as if the weight of what had happened was too much for him. Now he said:

'What are you going to do now, Captain Dawlish?'

'Get some sleep,' said Dawlish. 'My head's like a ball of fluff at the moment, and I can't think straight. I—' he hesitated. 'Oh, damn! I wonder if Tim arranged for that other flat?'

‘What’s the matter with 16a?’ demanded Felicity.

Dawlish looked at her, heavy-eyed. He did not even smile.

‘As you say,’ he said. ‘What’s the matter with 16a? Drive along, sweetheart.’

‘We’re already there,’ she said.

‘Oh. Nice work.’ Again he stifled a yawn, but he forced himself to speak to Montgomery. ‘Where would you like to be taken? The Clarion?’

‘My own flat is just round the corner,’ said Montgomery. ‘But I must make a report. I—’ he, too, stifled a yawn, whilst Beresford put in:

‘I’ll look after the Colonel, Pat. You get inside, you’re done up.’ It was true, and Dawlish did not try to fight against the craving for sleep. He was only vaguely aware of Felicity going into the flat with him, Felicity taking off his shoes, Felicity covering him with an eiderdown.

He slept.

Felicity waited for Beresford. He had taken Montgomery and Julia to Julia’s flat above the shop in Brake Street; where, Montgomery told him, they had an unofficial office.

‘He wants to see Pat at ten sharp in the morning,’ Ted said to Felicity.

Felicity stared. ‘Did he actually say *sharp*?’

Beresford grinned. ‘He did. A very didactic little gentleman, the Colonel. How is our hero?’

Felicity smiled.

‘Sleeping off two fires, two explosions, a long train journey and some degree of worry, Ted.’

‘I can understand it all except the worry,’ grinned Ted. ‘I wonder where Tim is?’

He did not wonder for long.

Trivett and Tim arrived at the flat twenty minutes later, when

Felicity—at Ted's urgent suggestion—had at last gone to bed. Trivett was not in a good humour. He had been unable to find who had seen Bray put the call through from the private phone box at the Clarion, and although he had made exhaustive inquiries, he had discovered no trace of evidence that Bray had been staying at the hotel.

Tim had told him that the Eire envoy had given the Clarion as his address. Trivett had been annoyed not only because there was no trace of the man, but because Bray had elected to spend his first night in London on his own.

Ted Beresford frowned, thought of Dawlish, wondered how much that large man would tell the policeman, and then decided that there was no object in keeping silent; Pat would have to give the whole story in the morning. He sufficed himself with telling Trivett what had happened at the flat, and later at the St. John's Wood house.

Trivett was silent as he listened.

'It was the easiest thing in the world,' said Ted. 'We were all three in the lounge with no one else about, when the door opened and the chauffeur came in. Felicity and I could have faded out right there—I would have put my shirt on the chauffeur and Bray not turning up.'

'Why?' asked Trivett.

'Pat will tell you in the morning,' said Ted blandly. 'Anyhow, Pell—as he was apparently called—had a gun. We hadn't. Wisdom indicated that we did as we were told. I was planning to push the gentleman off the fire-escape when the explosion came outside, and I lost what chance I had. There were two more tough-looking beggars outside,' Ted added apologetically. 'I didn't feel it was the right moment for starting a rough-house.'

'And then?' asked Trivett: the Chief Inspector's thin face

suggested that he was not only a puzzled but a very disturbed man.

'We were driven to the St. John's Wood house, taken downstairs, and treated to a considerable amount of threat. Felicity was hobbled—apparently Bray had an idea that he could use her to persuade Pat to talk.'

'About what?'

'He appeared to have an idea that Pat had been in the business for some time.'

'I'm beginning to wonder that myself,' said Trivett grimly.

'Well, you needn't. He hasn't.'

Trivett brushed a hand through his hair. Beresford, who knew him well, had never known him so worried and depressed. And that was understandable; the man he was to guard from the next morning onwards was almost certainly dead. The delegation from Eire had lost its leader, and—more important from the strict police angle—its leader had proved himself no more than a crook who worked on a very ambitious scale.

Ted smiled as he rested a hand on the Chief Inspector's shoulder.

'Quit worrying about it, Bill. Let the diplomatists get their tongues tied up explaining it away. It's not your pigeon.'

'I'm beginning to wonder whose pigeon it is,' said Trivett gloomily, but he asked no more questions and left the flat soon afterwards. Tim Jeremy, cheered by the evidence that Pat's hunch about Julia was wrong, volunteered to take a spell of four hours on guard, for there was a possibility that there would be trouble.

There was none at 16a Jermyn Street.

But there was much fluttering in Whitehall that night.

The resident Eire minister telephoned to Dublin, Chief Inspector Trivett made statements, Colonel Montgomery made more statements. Dublin was finally convinced that its special envoy had acted in a way for which an apology was essential; a new envoy would be speedily appointed. Meanwhile, all possible information regarding the activities of Sebastian Bray would be appreciated.

Trivett and Montgomery, Julia Dawnay, officials at various ministries, worked not only late into the night but well past dawn to get a statement through with unrivalled speed. The fluttering in Whitehall thereafter subsided. The Rt. Hon. Morton Arkwright flew to Dublin, *incognito* to talk with Irish ministers.

By mid-afternoon he had telephoned a pleasing report.

Eire was as concerned about the mystery of Sebastian Bray as Whitehall. Eire, in fact, was prepared to be very accommodating. By the evening the radio and the press announced that: 'negotiations between Great Britain and Eire were progressing with great cordiality. The special envoy, Sebastian Bray, had been recalled but another would take his place immediately. It was to be Mr. David St. John, known to be well-disposed towards Great Britain'. The oft-dreamed of co-operation was now a mere matter of practical politics.

Or it appeared to be, until on his arrival by air at a London airport in company with Arkwright, Mr. David St. John was assassinated, dying instantaneously from three bullet wounds. The assassin escaped.

CHAPTER SEVENTEEN

REPERCUSSIONS

Dawlish learned of the tragedy while he was at 16a Jermyn Street eating, at long last, one of Felicity's grills. It was an excellent grill, the kind often dreamed of in war-time England, but seldom consumed. Luckily, it was all but finished before the telephone rang.

Dawlish heard Julia's voice, and he did not like the note of anxiety in it.

'Captain Dawlish, can you come to my Brake Street flat at once? Colonel Montgomery is here—and others.'

'Am I wanted alone?' demanded Dawlish.

'Not necessarily.' She was speaking quickly, but he paused when Dawlish asked:

'What's the trouble?

Then she told him. Dawlish assured her that he and Tim would go round without delay. Ted, he had decided quickly, would remain with Felicity.

Ted said quietly:

'So you were right, Pat.'

Dawlish looked at him, his face seeming to have grown gaunt and strained.

'About it being the beginning of the trouble? Oh, yes, I was right. Sebastian Bray was no more than a second-in-command, perhaps even a third. This business isn't being run by big shot crooks of the Al Capone type, believe me.'

Felicity drew a deep breath.

'What *is* going on in that head of yours, Pat?'

'Too much, darling. From the start I've thought that most of this affair has been phoney. Even Julia, although Tim doesn't subscribe to that. Eh, Tim?'

Tim Jeremy stared, too taken by surprise to be aggrieved.

'Surely you've given that idea up by now?'

'Yes and no,' said Dawlish. 'Julia knows a good deal that she hasn't told us. So does Montgomery. And Arkwright, Fayre, and probably others. My dear Timothy,' went on Dawlish, resting a hand on his friend's arm. 'I'm not suggesting that Julia's a modern Delilah: I'm just saying that from the start we've been led up the garden path. It isn't a fresh idea: I thought it when we were in Room 13 last night. You two,' he went on, looking from Tim to Ted, 'should have had much the same suspicion. First, Julia was on the train to make sure that we weren't watched. Second Julia had been up north and thought it a good opportunity to look us over. When Montgomery told us that, he made a brave effort to correct himself—you remember he talked first about "not being watched", then the accident of Julia being up north, and finally he hastily compromised between the two. However, you obviously missed the inference.'

'No, not quite,' said Ted. 'I thought Montgomery was making sure he didn't tell us too much.'

'And he was,' said Dawlish grimly. 'But the whole business was upside down. A mysterious liaison officer who is in touch with the Ministry of Propaganda digs out three junior officers who have been active in pre-war days, promotes them above the heads of the Secret Service and/or the Secret Branch at Scotland Yard, and gives them a *carte blanche*.' He paused. 'I didn't believe it for a moment.'

Ted looked at him bewilderedly.

'Then what did you believe? And why did you keep it to yourself?'

'I couldn't think of a better story,' admitted Dawlish, 'but I've had an idea what was behind it, and I think I'm proved right now. We were the Aunt Sallies—you put 'em up, we'll knock 'em down, spirit. They knew, or suspected, that Sebastian Bray was not a nice man. They wanted him investigated. They did not want anyone with the remotest official connection implicated. So some bright spark had the idea of giving us special leave, putting us on the job and letting us go our own sweet way. They hoped we would get some results, but if we didn't, and if Bray kicked up a stink, we would be the scapegoats. How far they would have gone along with us I don't know, but you can take it from me that we would have smarted for it. The official story would have been that we acted as private individuals, on leave, and quite without authority.'

Felicity tapped ash from her cigarette.

'The brutes,' she said.

'Well, it has this to be said for it,' said Dawlish dispassionately. 'We were excellent bait. Our past was against us.' He smiled, but his eyes did not look amused. 'That was what I made of the situation within an hour of coming away, and that is why I didn't tell them what I'd done to Bray—or where I'd put him. I thought it would be better if we coped with Bray on our own. It's worked out more or less as I hoped. Bray's been proved such an utter rogue that Eire obviously can't raise much of a protest—in fact, from what Montgomery told us earlier in the day, they're badly upset in Dublin. So we get through.'

Ted eased his collar.

'*Phe-ew!* Life is tough and life is earnest.'

'I say, Pat.' Tim was sober-faced. 'Do you think Julia lied when she said she didn't know Bray?'

'I do. I think the whole story was phoney. I think that Montgomery was snooty when I argued a bit, particularly when I pointed out the idiocy of letting Julia travel about alone. Julia either was followed all the time, without results—there were a lot of people at King's Cross, remember, and we were well-watched, although no one visited us apart from Bray and Pell—or else it was considered wiser to let Bray carry on after his threats to her. The idea then was: Bray can do no wrong. Trivett was worried about him—there was nothing he could do about Bray "at the moment", he said, and the qualification was instructive. Oh, yes, we were the Aunt Sallies, and we did our part well.'

'But why the hell didn't you say so last night?' demanded Beresford. 'I'd like to write it all out and ram it down Montgomery's throat. And Arkwright's, too, for that matter.'

Dawlish smiled.

'Bull-at-a-gate methods aren't always useful, Ted. I saw no reason why we shouldn't play a part, while looking around for the sober facts. In this we haven't had a lot of luck. But we've had some. Arkwright isn't a man who would put over a hoax for the sake of it. His presence, and Fayre's, mean that the authorities really are worried. But not as worried as they appeared to be in some ways. For instance, I wondered how Bray had learned about us: obviously no serious attempt was made to stop him knowing. In fact, I should say that Julia was on that train to focus Bray's attention on us.'

Tim moved restlessly.

'You make it sound so damned convincing,' he muttered.

'What are you going to do now?' Felicity asked abruptly.

'See Montgomery,' answered Dawlish. 'When I've heard what he has to say I'll decide. This time, if we work, we work in the open.'

'What do you make of it?' asked Tim.

'David St. John's death?' asked Dawlish, and he was silent as he slipped into his coat. 'I think that someone is very anxious that Eire gets upset.'

'Berlin, you mean?'

'It could be. It needn't be. Hitler isn't the only rogue in Europe, and there are people with a good bellyful of hate for us in Ireland. Ready, Tim?'

'Aye, aye, sir.'

'Good.' Dawlish bent to kiss Felicity: 'I haven't tasted a grill like that in months, sweetheart. I'll be back for some more.'

She laughed as he went out, with Tim, and closed the door.

In Julia Dawnay's flat, above the small salon, Montgomery and Julia were waiting; and with them was Fayre. That under-secretary's genial and rubicund face was set in lines of anxiety, and Colonel Montgomery gave the impression that he had grown years older in twenty-four hours.

He nodded brusquely.

'Glad to see you're all right, Dawlish. I won't forget last night's business in a hurry. Good evening, Jeremy.' He was sitting at a desk, flanked by the comfortably ensconced Fayre and Julia. Only hard chairs remained for the visitors.

'You understand the immensity of the crime which has been committed?' Montgomery asked.

'More or less,' said Dawlish.

'More or less! That assassination is one of the most grievous injuries that this country has sustained for—'

'Now, come,' said Dawlish comfortably. 'We don't have to talk like copy-books, do we? Eire has been unfriendly enough in the past. This won't make her declare for Germany. It's a damned nuisance, but except to people who know St. John it's not a tragedy.'

Fayre jerked his head up.

'Do you quite understand what it means, Dawlish?'

'I think so,' said Dawlish. 'Someone is throwing a spanner into the works. Eire must see that as well as we do. Public opinion might get a little inflamed, but de Valera isn't going to think that we instigated the crime. If he did think so we might have something to worry about, but he's not a nitwit.'

'Your manner is somewhat abrupt,' Montgomery said stiffly.

Dawlish shrugged. 'Velvet gloves take time, and are sometimes misleading.'

He had judged from Montgomery's manner that there was to be no exchange of confidences. He had hardly expected that there would be although he had thought it just possible that he would be told the truth, and asked—or even told—to work on a new basis. He had concluded that was not to be the case, and he did not propose to hold his punches.

'To go on from there,' Dawlish said dryly. 'I propose here and now to tell you what I think of your attitude towards me and my friends. It isn't complimentary. We were lucky enough to prove that Bray was a rogue, and one who couldn't be whitewashed, but that wasn't due to you, was it?'

Montgomery's breath was coming a little faster than normal, while the under-secretary's fingers began to drum on the arm of his chair.

'What do you mean?' rapped Montgomery, recovering his poise with a visible effort.

Dawlish told him. At the end of it there was utter silence, then Montgomery cleared his throat.

'All right, Dawlish. There is no object in denial. It was hoped that you would get some results, it was believed that you would attract Bray's attention while inquiries were being made about him, and you succeeded. We have made one or two discoveries. We have, for instance, found reasonable proof that Bray is not associated with any Fifth Column. We do not know what he is doing precisely, but we must find out. Undoubtedly he instigated the assassination this afternoon.'

Dawlish stared at him.

Soreness at the trick which had been served him, at Montgomery's manner, at the raw deal, quite disappeared. He could not keep his mind off one vital thing, but it was some seconds before he put it into words. Then he spoke quietly enough:

'Did you say "is doing"?'

'Yes,' said Montgomery.

'But the fire at St. John's Wood?'

'There were no traces of burned bodies,' said Montgomery. 'I had that report in an hour or more ago. But since then I have proof that Bray is alive—he was seen travelling in the direction of the airport this afternoon, though not actually at the landing-field itself.' The Colonel's voice dropped a little. 'You are prepared to continue your argument with him I trust, Captain Dawlish?'

Both he and Fayre looked hard at Dawlish as they waited for a reply.

CHAPTER EIGHTEEN

PROPER BASIS?

Dawlish appeared to hesitate for a long time.

It was clear that Montgomery, Fayre and Julia were hanging on his words, and he saw no reason why they should not continue so to do.

The escape of Bray and Pell was a shock.

He had argued with himself during the day that they could not have escaped, although he knew that there had been a time lag just sufficient for that to happen. As soon as Beresford had been discovered by the man who had been in the upper part of the house, someone must have hurried to the cellar, released the two men, and carried them to safety.

The explosion had been caused by a time bomb.

That there had always been a possibility in the mind of Bray—or whoever was backing the business—of the need for destroying the house had been apparent the moment it had gone up.

The contents; what had they been?

It was clear enough that there had been records of the organization in the house, but there was one factor which Dawlish could not understand. Bray had been frightened of letting the house be blown up; Bray, in fact, had apparently been prepared to bargain Dawlish's life for the safety of the house. But someone, as yet unknown, had destroyed the place swiftly, making a decision which must have been instantaneous. It had not been Bray; and for that reason Dawlish had assumed that there was someone more important than Bray, behind it. He had clung to that theory throughout the day, but the news that Bray was alive gave him cause to doubt it.

Could the red-haired man have recovered consciousness in time to have pressed the necessary switch—or to have given the order for the switch to be pressed?

There was no way of being sure, and Dawlish forced himself to put the thought out of his mind. The immediate issue had little to do with Bray.

Fayre broke the long silence.

'Tell me, Captain Dawlish, if you realized something of the real nature of the work we had for you, why did you not say so at the time?'

Dawlish smiled. 'I can answer that one. I knew there was bother, or you wouldn't have gone to such lengths. Had I proved crabby, you would have regretted politely that I could be of no assistance, and—' his smile widened into a grin—'if you had spent six benighted months in a camp that was under water half the time you would know what I mean.'

'Quite so,' said Fayre, and his eyes twinkled.

'You have not yet answered my question, Captain Dawlish.' Colonel Montgomery's voice was crisp and precise. Odd, mused Dawlish, that he should have made such a point of informality while being the most formal of men. For that matter, Fayre was acting like a politician whose party had told him not to allow his personal exuberance or enthusiasms to get the better of him.

'I'm considering it,' said Dawlish. 'I'd like to see Bray finished, gentlemen, but I'd also like to work on an equitable basis.'

'I don't quite follow you.'

'I was afraid you wouldn't,' said Dawlish gently. 'An equitable basis, sir, appears to me to be one in which I am told of the dangers which I am to face, and all of the known difficulties. I am not speaking from any feeling of annoyance, I assure you. In pre-war days I would have taken a chance, and gone my own sweet way. But the war being about us, that is less possible. Understandably, enthusiastic young men with a sense of rough justice cannot so easily take the law into their own hands. The penalties are greater. The police have only to murmur "special regulations" and clap such men in jail to cool their heels. In short, the individual has no particular privileges outside the vital civil liberties which are hardly those which would affect me if I continued the game with Sebastian Bray. Is that clearer?'

Montgomery drew a sharp breath.

'I think so. Perhaps you will be even more precise.'

'Certainly. How much of the original story that you gave us is true?'

'Virtually all of it, except where it concerned you personally.' Fayre broke in, to Montgomery's obvious annoyance. 'The situation between Great Britain and Eire is delicate,' Fayre went on, 'and the latest crime may well sabotage our relationship, despite your assumption that the matter is not so serious as we would like to make out.' Fayre's eyes were laughing; Dawlish warmed to the man. 'From the beginning we suspected that Bray was not what he made himself out to be, but the strictest inquiries in Dublin merely confirmed that he *was* the special envoy. He had an unsavoury background, and yet Eire chose to appoint him. Our difficulties increased, but now that he has been forced to come into the open—thanks of course to you—in some measure they are alleviated. But we *must* get the murderer of David St. John.'

'Ye-es,' said Dawlish. 'And presumably that's Bray.'

'It appears so.'

'It could be,' admitted Dawlish. 'I hope he hasn't got nine lives. However, to get back to a basis—how do I work?'

'You have a *carte blanche*.'

'I had one before,' said Dawlish dryly.

'Try to forget that,' said Fayre, and he was no longer smiling. 'Quite frankly, Dawlish, Colonel Montgomery, Mr. Arkwright and myself thought that your ability had been considerably over-rated. We no longer think that. We feel that you can get results, and we must have them quickly.'

'Good,' said Dawlish briskly. 'I'll want four special permits signed by the Home Secretary and countersigned by the Commander-in-Chief Home Forces. The permits will have to give me free access to and from any part of the country, and a *visa* to go out of the country and to enter it again, if necessary. I shall want a similar permit from the police, so that if at any time I want local police to act they will do so without waiting to confirm my authority. Can that be done?'

'Why four?' asked Montgomery.

'It will be done,' said Fayre.

'The whys and wherefores are mine,' said Dawlish gently. 'I told you before, sir, that there is a leakage in high places, and the less known about my movements and intentions the better. In any case, I don't know what I shall be doing from one hour to the next—you will have noticed that the conditions change abruptly. There is another thing. I should like Miss Dawnay to be appointed to co-operate with me.'

Montgomery looked at Julia: she nodded. Montgomery cleared his throat and said:

'All right, Captain Dawlish.'

'Good,' said Dawlish briskly.

'Have you any idea where you are going to start?' asked Fayre.

'Not the faintest.' Dawlish smiled, while Ted and Julia stood up. 'Is this flat to be considered headquarters?' he asked.

'Yes,' said Montgomery.

'Right. I'll appreciate it if you will get those permits along to my flat—16a Jermyn Street will find me for the time being—just as soon as possible.'

Five minutes later he was stepping into Ted Beresford's car, Julia beside him. Ted spread his large bulk into the tonneau.

'Nice of you to help,' Dawlish said somewhat sardonically, and Julia laughed lightly.

'You have a way with you, haven't you?'

'One which I trust has shaken up Montgomery's formality. Who on earth thought of appointing him as liaison officer?'

'I don't know. It's a comparatively new appointment.'

'What does "comparatively" mean exactly?'

'Within the last six months.' Julia hesitated. She went on at last:

'Mr. Dawlish—'

'Pat to you.'

'Well then, Pat, my father held a similar position before Colonel Montgomery. He—my father—and I worked up the *salon* as a blind. Actually it proved far more successful than we expected, and turned out to be an ideal meeting place for unofficial contacts.'

Dawlish nodded, fearful that the wrong word would break the thread of reminiscence.

'Officially, my father was the military attache to the Ministry of Propaganda,' Julia went on. 'Actually he was in the Intelligence Service. The fashion salon received a dozen agents, and their reports, each week. Sometimes more. I acted as confidential secretary, but I did very little active work.'

'I see,' said Dawlish.

Ted was no longer sprawling, but sitting forward so that he could hear what Julia was saying. That she contrived to tell her story without any trace of histrionics, made it all the more impressive.

'Go on,' Dawlish murmured.

Although she smiled there was a touch of sadness in the girl's eyes, in her voice. 'Father always urged the strengthening of our News Service abroad, and nine months ago he was appointed by Mr. Arkwright as the Foreign Propaganda Director. It was soon after that that difficulties began in Eire and other places—the slowing down and the misdirection of the delivery of goods. You know about it, I think.'

'Yes,' said Dawlish.

'One school of thought believed that nothing could be done beyond making representations to the neutral countries concerned, but my father thought differently, and his opinion carried. He argued that only certain cargoes went astray, and that orders for the misdirection started from England.'

'Yes,' said Dawlish again.

'He and I began to work on that assumption,' said Julia speaking more quickly, 'and about a month afterwards I first saw Bray. I suspected he had some part in the business, and I followed it up. When I was trying to find out where he lived, he called to see me. He told me that if I continued to do this, he would kill my father.'

Dawlish took his eyes off the road for a moment to look at the girl, and he saw that she was staring straight ahead of her, her lips compressed, her chin raised a little.

'I didn't stop,' Julia said simply, 'and father was murdered.

It was hushed up—they gave it out that he had been killed by "enemy action". She uttered a short, sharp laugh, and in it there was a world of bitterness. 'Colonel Montgomery was appointed in father's place, and I kept my original job. Montgomery has been very good,' she added, 'in many ways. Behind that stiff front he's clever. If he thinks it necessary he will cut through red-tape ruthlessly and get down to it. It was he who suggested using you. Anyhow, that's beside the point. The next time I saw Bray was at King's Cross. I had come up to see you on the train—I had a colleague with me—'

'Who looked through our luggage,' said Dawlish.

She was startled. 'Did you realize that? It was one of the Colonel's ideas; he wanted your luggage checked, I don't know why. Anyhow, I saw Bray at the station, and then when I reached Room 13 I not only learned that Bray was the delegate from Eire, but that nothing could openly be done against him. I know we told you a farrago of nonsense about him in some ways, but we had no time to prepare a better story. We'd brought you down to work against Bray, and then we couldn't allow that. It was—' she paused.

'Call it awkward,' Dawlish said dryly. 'All right, Julia, it clears up a lot that was misty before. And now we'll get ready for the second hunt of Mr. Bray.'

'Ye-es,' said Julia. 'But why didn't you want information about the assassination? Isn't the airfield the place to start?'

'Since the assassin wasn't caught, no,' said Dawlish. 'It's police work, and I'm no policeman, thank the Lord. I don't want to go round chasing hares and red herrings. It's too tiring.'

'But what are you going to do?'

Dawlish drew the car into the kerb outside 16a Jermyn Street, and switched off the engine.

He looked sideways at Julia Dawnay.

'I have a greater faith than Mohammed,' he said amiably. 'He went to the mountain—I'm going to wait for the mountain to come to me. In the person of Bray or his underlings—or over-lords, for that matter.'

'I don't understand you,' said Julia.

'You will,' said Dawlish. 'We're now going in for a snack, and then all of us are going for a little spin into the country.' He smiled. 'We'll be followed, or I'll resign,' he said; and she knew that he believed it, and wondered why he could be so sure.

CHAPTER NINETEEN

FULL BLAST

Some fifty miles from London, in a Hampshire district which knew little of air-raids beyond the droning of passing aircraft, was a house known as White Lodge.

The name no longer suited it.

Immediately after the declaration of war, the owner had brought a small army of workmen from London, who first camouflaged the white paint and then constructed an air-raid shelter of a kind calculated to offer absolute security. The workmen had been busy for three months, and there were rumours that Mr. Fesell proposed to make his shelter a public one. In point of fact, he did nothing of the kind, for it was soon made abundantly clear that his own safety was his sole concern.

He was known as an archeologist who spent many months of each year abroad; it was also known that he took his work, both literary and practical, most seriously.

Tall and spare, he was little more than forty, but his sharp nose and thin lipless mouth, his weak indeterminate chin, robbed him of such youth that he had.

He was reputed to live a blameless life.

Clearly he was wealthy—he ran three cars, including a Rolls and a Daimler—he had a staff of seven indoor servants and nine outdoor, somewhat more than his hundred-and-eleven acres of land needed.

When he was asked to take evacuees at White Lodge, in the early days of the war, he pointed out that a bachelor archeologist's home was hardly suitable for children, nevertheless he offered to house his eight outdoor servants, thus leaving four cottages, fully furnished and equipped, at the disposal of the authorities.

This plan was acclaimed with great enthusiasm, Julian Fesell's generosity being cited as that of an ideal country gentleman fully conscious of his responsibilities.

Then Mr. Fesell's warm-heartedness displayed itself in other ways. Talking to the vicar one day he said that he had a host of friends and relatives in the larger cities, and he thought of offering them hospitality. It would not only give them safety but it would increase the prosperity of the village.

So from time to time people arrived at White Lodge. If there was anything remarkable about it, it was the fact that they appeared to be more-or-less of an age—somewhere between thirty-five and forty, and mostly men. There were, however, some women, and Lucille Lefroy was among them.

Her first appearance in the village created something of a stir, for she was beautiful. She also busied herself among the evacuees, giving small parties for them.

Mr. Julian Fesell allowed it to be known that he was glad his niece was making herself popular, and that he had never before realized what a difference a woman made in a home.

Some of the twenty-odd people who lived in the Lodge—a house with some fifty rooms—travelled daily to London to work. Others appeared to work on the premises. Yet others appeared to have no profession or occupation, and busied themselves in the village. They formed a patrol of the Home Guard. They formed an A.R.P. unit of unrivalled efficiency. There was no better-prepared village in all England, claimed the vicar and the squire—Sir Mortimer Fairhaven—and that was generally conceded. It became a show-place. Newspapers starred Mr. Fesell and his remarkable arrangements. But one thing did not pass entirely unobserved; no one was ever invited to see the underground shelter which he had had built at such expense.

Thus Mr. Julian Fesell, and his 'niece', Miss Lucille Lefroy, and his guests, one of which, red-haired and blue-eyed, Dawlish would have recognized as Sebastian Bray.

Very few telephone calls were made to or from White Lodge, but in the underground rooms there were several telephones, some extensions of the Post Office system, others house-telephones which enabled Fesell to keep in close contact with the rest of the house, for it was here he worked.

On the morning that Dawlish was sleeping late, and on the day which was later to see the murder of David St. John, the telephone nearest Fesell's hand rang out. He lifted it.

'Yes, who is that?'

A sharp voice answered him.

'It's Abel. I must see you at once.'

'Oh, Abel.' Fesell appeared to cogitate. 'I think I can manage that, my friend. Will you have anyone with you?'

'Yes, the usual.'

'I see.' Fesell appeared to be even more thoughtful. 'I won't be prepared for you all until—let me see—eight o'clock this evening. Come in at the side door. I'll be delighted to have a talk then, delighted.'

He closed down, but the expression in his dark eyes did not

suggest particular delight. Tight-lipped, he pressed a bell which was one of eight set in a panel beneath the top of the desk.

The door of the room opened.

There were, in fact, three doors—two of them, camouflaged as windows, operated by electricity. The main door was of oak, and iron-studded; it opened slowly.

Lucille entered.

She moved with the swinging grace which had caused some village wit to nickname her Mae West. Had Dawlish seen her, he would have been considerably startled by her eyes; they were amber, very wide-set and expressive.

Apparently she was fond of her 'uncle' for she said: 'Hallo, darling, you're early this morning.' She sat on the corner of his desk, resting a hand over his.

'What is it?'

Fesell said very slowly:

'Bray failed. The London house was destroyed.'

She did not move, but the hand covering his tightened.

'*Destroyed*,' she whispered.

'The blundering fool,' said Fesell slowly. 'The damned—blundering—fool.' He was silent for a moment, then went on: 'Abel telephoned. He is coming tonight, with the others, and that means they had to get away from the house. If it had not been destroyed he would have told me.'

'Where is Bray?'

'Abel did not say.' Fesell pushed his chair back and paced the room. 'It is this man Dawlish,' he added abruptly.

'But—'

'It must be Dawlish! Nothing went wrong before. We had them fooled. I was always afraid of Dawlish, a blundering idiot without any sense of danger or fear—they are the dangerous kind. It is impossible to outwit them, nor can they be pushed

aside, you can only stop them. And Bray did not stop Dawlish.'
There was silence for some seconds, and then he said abruptly:
'I read all I could about Dawlish the moment I knew he was
coming here. He has not been unsuccessful, he is not wholly
a fool. I thought that Bray could disarm him through the
woman—Bray failed. God knows how, but he failed.'

'What does he know?' Lucille asked evenly.

'I have no idea. Whatever it is,' said Fesell more slowly, 'he
will keep to himself, that type always does. There is a complete
record of his previous activities—he works without consulting
the authorities unless they force his hand, and I do not think
they have done that yet. We must stop him quickly.'

'How?' asked Lucille.

Fesell stared at her, his dark eyes brooding.

'I do not know. He must be watched, of course—I have a
report from Keltzer that he has not yet left the flat in Jermyn
Street where he is staying. There is time for you to get up there
I think, Lucille.'

'What can I do?'

'Get Dawlish away from London,' said Fesell sharply. 'You
can handle it as you think best. Get him away.'

'I'll do that,' said Lucille, but she hesitated. 'What is going to
happen about Bray?'

'I am not sure. Abel would not have telephoned had Bray
been able to speak himself. We must assume that Bray can no
longer play the part we had worked out for him. Curse him!'
said Julian Fesell, and the words were uttered with such inten-
sity that they made it seem as if a curse had really fallen on the
head of Sebastian Bray. 'We must act quickly. I shall keep a close
watch. If Dublin sends another man—'

'Yes?' she said.

'We must kill him. St. John is the most likely envoy. His death will give us the time in which to work.' He turned abruptly. 'Get to London, Lucille. Do not telephone unless absolutely necessary. Bring Dawlish and the others with him here, if you can, but after dark. If you can't, make quite sure he cannot make further trouble. It is,' added Fesell slowly, 'a very different proposition from operating against the police and the secret service. Dawlish works by no rules. I am relying on you, Lucille.'

She laughed a little, but it was not a pleasant sound; and then she touched his cheek for a moment, and left the room.

CHAPTER TWENTY

ABEL

Tim Jeremy and Felicity were sitting in the lounge when Dawlish, Ted and Julia entered the room.

'Hallo, hallo,' said Tim, his eyes lighting up as they swept over Julia. 'Welcome home, little stranger. You did promise to look us up, didn't you?'

'Wasn't that a long time ago?' asked Julia.

'Any time's the right time. Eh, Pat?'

'You are an oaf,' declared Patrick, good-humouredly. 'Julia's enlisted with us,' he added.

'Oh, nice work!'

'In a working capacity only,' said Dawlish with assumed severity. 'Business and pleasure aren't mixing, my son.'

'Under such circumstances all business is pleasure,' declared Timothy.

Silently Beresford filled two tankards, Julia shaking her head at his inquiring glance. 'It's a barbaric hour to drink beer, admittedly,' he murmured, 'but we don't always get the chance. Here's how.'

'Down the hatch,' said Tim.

'Here's to the mountain's quick arrival,' said Dawlish.

'What mountain?' asked Felicity.

Dawlish eyed her smilingly.

'The Bray mountain, darling. I may or may not be right, but I have a feeling. A pleasing feeling,' he added. 'Did any of you know that we were followed to and from Brake Street?' Julia and Ted regarded him with sudden soberness.

'Out with it,' said Ted at last.

Dawlish motioned to the window.

'There was a cab at the end of the street when we started, and there was a cab on our tail most of the way. It was nicely done. I don't think I would have realized it but for the glasses.'

'Talk sense,' demanded Ted Beresford.

'Steel-rimmed glasses, small, cotton used for mending, taxi-driver at King's Cross—' went on Dawlish dreamily.

'Great Scott!' exclaimed Beresford.

'The penny's dropped at last,' acknowledged Dawlish, with an exaggerated sigh of relief. 'He followed us, there's no doubt of it, and he's outside now. Ted, slip along to the old flat—come back with a case as if you'd been to fetch something—and see what happens.'

Beresford finished his beer with a flourish, and rose.

'Very good, sir.'

Dawlish stepped to the window, in such a position that he would be unseen from the street. He saw the middle-aged cabby with the cotton-mended glasses sitting at the wheel of his cab, his flag down, an evening paper spread in front of him. No more normal, natural scene could be expected in London. But when Beresford left the front door the cabby looked up from his paper, Dawlish saw him reach for the handbrake. But the cab did not move, and the driver relaxed after a few seconds, picking up his paper again.

'Ted's reached the other flat,' said Dawlish, and he turned about, smiling to himself, clearly well-pleased. 'There's our mountain, friends, and if you want further evidence my guess is that we shall most certainly be followed when we go for a spin this evening.' He lit a cigarette. 'We'll let him sit for an hour while we eat, Felicity. That is if the larder will stand it.'

Felicity shook her head. 'I'm afraid it won't. I'm sending for some food from the restaurant.'

As she put the phone down, Beresford returned with an empty suit-case.

The taxi-driver remained in Jermyn Street.

One hour later, at half past six precisely, a little convoy of cars and cabs left the street. Tim had brought his Talbot, Beresford his Alvis. Dawlish had made the arrangements and Tim had blessed him.

'Tim and Julia together,' Dawlish had said, 'Felicity, Ted and I in the other bus. We'll get out on to the Great West Road, and as soon as we've a chance, we'll sandwich the cab. You'll keep in front, Tim, making for Staines. We'll drop behind. By then the gentleman will probably be worried.'

The plan was not difficult to carry out, but there was one thing Dawlish had not expected.

He first noticed the Austin 20 behind him after he had reached the Great West Road. A very lovely woman was driving it.

Dawlish had no objections to lovely women as such; on the contrary. But it occurred to him that a lovely with a mink coat carelessly flung in the back would, not normally, be travelling in a five-year old Austin. The value of the coat and the car were at variance. He argued with himself that he could be wrong in putting a sinister interpretation on the combination, but he could not get it out of his head.

Quite suddenly he pulled into a garage. The Austin passed quickly, then it slowed down a little.

Some distance ahead Tim had also slowed down.

Dawlish turned abruptly to Beresford:

'Watch the Austin, old man.'

Beresford and Felicity, their attention thus attracted, saw that the Austin travelled slowly until they passed it, and then kept pace. Ted smiled a little to himself.

'Spider number two,' he said. 'What made you think of her?'

'Her coat,' said Dawlish cryptically. 'Let's see. One in front, one behind, and Tim and Julia leading the way. I think we'll turn off in a few minutes.

'What about Tim?' asked Felicity.

'He should be able to look after himself,' said Dawlish. 'If he's surprised he shouldn't be.'

Dawlish slowed down at the approach to a by-road, put out his hand, and turned. He did not do it too quickly, for he wanted the car to follow him if that was the woman's intention, and there seemed little doubt of it.

She turned also.

'Nice going,' said Ted. 'What do we do now? Stop and hold her up? Or invite her to join the party?'

Felicity, who was staring into the mirror by Dawlish's head, spoke suddenly.

'She's going to pass.'

'Bless her heart,' said Dawlish. 'The old trick, or I'll eat my hat. She'll get past, then stop, and ask us sweetly for help.'

He deliberately slowed down, and waved Lucille Lefroy past.

She acknowledged the courtesy with a smile so natural that for the first time Felicity began to wonder whether Pat could be mistaken. For some quarter of a mile the road went straight, and then the Austin disappeared round a corner.

The faces of the two men hardened.

'Up to you, Ted,' said Dawlish, and Beresford quietly drew an automatic from his pocket. 'Be ready to duck, darling,' Dawlish added to Felicity.

Then slowly he rounded the bend.

His fear that there was to be shooting was not immediately justified, but his other guess was. The Austin was drawn up in the side of the road, and the woman was standing by the bonnet, which was raised. She looked up as the other car appeared, and again her smile, and her expression of relief, seemed perfectly natural.

Dawlish slowed down.

Their first look at Lucille Lefroy—except for the glimpses when she had been at the wheel—were comprehensive if short. They saw her beauty, and her air of helplessness, and Dawlish nearly laughed aloud; such tricks had been played since cars were first possessed by women drivers. He, too, acted naturally, although Beresford kept a hand in his pocket about his gun.

'Can we help?' asked Dawlish, genially.

'That's extremely good of you. I don't know what's the matter—it was going perfectly a few minutes ago.'

She looked straight at Dawlish, and he had one of the shocks of his life. There was something about her eyes, amber, far apart, that made him almost certain that he had seen her—or someone very like her—before. That they spelt danger, he had no doubt whatever.

It was as he bent over the engine of the Austin that he remembered where he had seen them.

Amber, wide apart, and soon to be closed for ever, they had been the eyes of the fair-haired man he had carried from his flat in Jermyn Street.

CHAPTER TWENTY-ONE

DAWLISH HAS AN IMPULSE

Dawlish fiddled with the carburettor. The smell of petrol was sharp in his nostrils as he tried to think clearly. He was surprised that he was so affected by the development, and even tried to dismiss his attitude as being unnecessarily alarmist.

He did not convince himself.

He did not believe that two people implicated in the same business and with the same unusual-coloured eyes were unrelated. Brother and sister might have similar eyes, or even cousins: strangers, almost certainly not.

He straightened up and looked into Lucille's face again; his second scrutiny confirmed his first impression.

'Did you try that?' he asked, pointing to the engine.

'Pulling up that little thing? No. What does it do?'

'It's the carburettor,' he explained carefully. 'It helps the petrol to make the car go. If it gets stuck or dried up there's a break in the flow of petrol. Therefore, no sparking. Therefore, a hold-up.' He smiled, and slipped into the driving-seat. He pulled the self-starter, and the engine picked up.

Lucille stared, wide-eyed.

'But that's incredible.'

'Yes, isn't it?'

It was then that Dawlish heard the drone of cars coming along the road in the direction he and Lucille had travelled. He turned sharply to Beresford.

'Dive on, Ted. Make it snappy.'

Lucille's lips parted.

'No time just now,' said Dawlish. He slipped out of Lucille's car, lifted her easily, and dumped her into the seat next to the driver's. He slipped in beside her as Beresford and Felicity drove past.

The engines of the approaching cars grew louder.

Dawlish let out the clutch, and eased off the brake of the Austin. Lucille said sharply:

'What does this mean? Stop at once!'

The car started off with a lurch, but he was twenty yards along the road before a powerful-looking car turned the corner. Two hundred yards in front of him the Talbot was going at high speed.

On Lucille's face there was something approaching hatred, and Dawlish saw her open her handbag.

He shot out his left hand, snatched the bag away: and on to his knees fell a small automatic.

He took a swift glance behind him.

There were two cars now, and in each there were three men.

He actually saw the guns.

In that moment his heart beat a trifle faster: if they began shooting he would not have a big chance of getting away: whether they would risk hitting the woman was the thing that mattered.

He did not think she would be quiet for long.

Her gun was under his heel. She would not be able to get it, and he was ready to fend off any attempt she made to get at the controls of the car. His foot pressed harder on the accelerator.

He saw the woman clench her fist, and knew she was going to strike him. He put out his left arm with a quick sudden movement that deceived her, put it about her shoulders and hugged her close to his side. It meant that he had only his right arm free for driving but it put her out of action.

Until she bit him.

The pain startled Dawlish, who momentarily lost his control of the wheel. The Austin lurched to one side, and he heard the squealing of brakes behind him.

Ahead, he saw Ted's car turn into a narrow lane.

As luck would have it the sudden lurch of the Austin had enabled him to gain nearly twenty yards; he was thirty or more from the nearest attacking car, and all three were swaying up and down, with speedometers quivering about the sixty mark, a suicidal speed on so narrow and uneven a road.

The Austin swept past the lane where Beresford had gone. He was travelling too fast to get any real idea of what was happening, but he was fairly sure of what Beresford would do.

Above the roar of the engines came the shooting.

He was thinking of Felicity; they would shoot back, of course, and he found himself praying for her. He slowed down, only a little; and then he heard a report louder than the rest.

He dared a glance over his shoulder.

He saw what had happened and could have shouted aloud for the joy of it. Ted had opened fire from the lane, and he had hit one of the wheels of the first crooks' car.

Dawlish saw the car lurching across the road.

He slowed down, quickly, jerking himself and the woman forward. As he applied the brake he heard the crash of the car behind him. Again he looked round, and he saw that the first car had crashed right across the road; the second could not hope to get past.

Beresford was still shooting. Dawlish could see him crouching in the tonneau of the Talbot. He smiled from sheer relief, and then he released the woman, whom he had been pressing to his side in an attempt to lessen her attack.

A quick fear went through him—a fear that he had suffocated her. She was purplish in the face, and the beauty that had been hers had gone. He grimaced, slipped out of the car, and lowered her across both seats. He could see then that she was breathing, but he knew she would not be conscious for at least ten or fifteen minutes.

He picked up the automatic and her handbag, searched for and found the door key of the Austin. Leaving one of the windows down, he locked her in the car.

By then bullets were flying his way.

Of the six men in the two cars, four were now in the field at the side of the road: one was lying by the fence, the sixth was nowhere in sight. Two of them were firing towards him, and two at Beresford.

Dawlish, carrying his service automatic, crouched low by the Austin, and returned the fire. He scored one hit in four shots, seeing a man stagger and then slowly drop to the ground. He fired twice more before the trio still on their feet turned and ran.

Dawlish waited until the fleeing men were out of shooting range then began to walk towards Beresford and Felicity.

She met him, smiling, clearly unhurt. Her hands gripped his forearm. He felt her trembling a little, and he put an arm about her. 'It must have looked grim once or twice,' he acknowledged. 'Nice work, Ted, you did what I prayed you'd do.'

'One of these days you'll pray in vain,' said Felicity with feeling. 'Why didn't you tell us what you thought was going to happen?'

Dawlish said ruefully:

'My dear, I hadn't a notion, though I should have had. The girl followed us, and was followed in turn by her bodyguard. She must have thought we were in the bag when we turned up here, and stopped. However, we didn't do so badly.'

'Is she all right?' asked Felicity.

'Provided she's alive and with her vocal cords in working order, that's all I ask,' Dawlish said repressively. 'Go and see what you can do for her. Here's her gun—it will about fit you.'

He watched her as she walked swiftly towards the Austin, then he and Beresford approached the smashed car.

The three men had escaped on foot—there was little or no chance of catching them. Dusk was falling over the countryside but there was enough light for Dawlish to see an approaching pedal-cyclist some half mile away.

The man drew nearer as Dawlish and Beresford reached the crooks' cars.

Both were entangled together.

'One unholy mess,' opined Beresford.

'More than one,' said Dawlish.

He was right, for, the driver of the first car had been crushed by the broken steering-wheel: he was dead. So also was the man by the fence; shot through the temple. But the third man, whom Dawlish had winged, was not only alive but conscious; he was trying to crawl away, and Dawlish had a quick appreciation of the man's courage.

'Get him, Ted,' he said, and then turned to the cyclist.

It was a big, burly, red-faced Home Guard, who held his rifle a little in front of him and looked prepared to use it. Dawlish smiled, but it had no effect.

'Put that gun down,' said the Home Guard sharply.

Dawlish shrugged and slipped his gun into his holster. 'How much did you see?'

'Plenty,' said the Home Guard, gruffly. 'You can do all your talking later, mister.' Looking past the man Dawlish saw at least a dozen Home Guard approaching, not in a bunch but widely separated, as men might be who were stalking dangerous quarry. A dozen rifles were cocked, and Dawlish had a momentary spasm of apprehension.

For the first time he really had some idea of the range and capability of the volunteer army.

An oldish, grey-haired man holding a revolver snapped an order, and almost immediately Dawlish was encircled by men.

He saw also that Felicity, by the Austin, was in the same predicament. He stared at the officer, and then he laughed; he could not help it.

'So this amuses you, does it?' asked the officer, and he was looking at the two dead men. 'Green, remove their guns.'

The burly cyclist did so in a movement which suggested he had done similar things before. Dawlish forced back a sudden feeling of irritation, and wished that the permits he had asked for had arrived before he had left Jermyn Street. He said soberly:

'Spare me a couple of minutes on your own, sir, will you?'

'I will not,' said the officer.

Dawlish hesitated, and then a man came running from the second patrol; he poured out his story about a woman half-strangled in the car, and the officer's gaze grew more frosty. He gave orders quickly, and men sprang to obey; it could not have been done more efficiently in the regular army.

'Two of you remove the woman. Take her to Lanley Hospital and see that she has all the attention necessary. Green, you and your patrol will start to clear the wreckage. You,' added the officer to Dawlish and Beresford, 'are coming with me.'

Dawlish stared at him.

Through his mind there flashed the difficulty of convincing

the man of what had happened, and why: he could picture the woman being taken to hospital, recovering and escaping; and he knew that it must not happen, that she must not have the chance. But he was far less confident as he faced that small, grey-haired officer than when he had faced Sebastian Bray in the cellar at John's Wood.

CHAPTER TWENTY-TWO

SHALL SHE GO?

Dawlish eyed the officer for some seconds: he met a cold gaze which suggested the other had already formed a judgment of what had happened, and that it was not complimentary to Dawlish. Then the large man said:

'You're being somewhat arbitrary, aren't you?'

'I am detaining you for questioning,' the officer answered.

'As you like, but please accede to my request that the injured woman comes with us.'

'I have already given instructions—'

Dawlish let himself go.

For some time he quite forgot his earlier appreciation of the speed and thoroughness of the rounding-up. It might have been that the strain of the fight, while it had lasted, had been greater than he had yet shown, and his diatribe owed something to that.

He did not raise his voice; he did not need to. A faint colour rose on the officer's cheeks, and strained expressions began to show on the faces of the guards, as the authoritative voice, cutting and decisive, went on.

Dawlish paused at last, but went on before anyone else had recovered sufficiently to speak.

'And now perhaps, sir, you will accede to a reasonable request and take the injured woman with us. If you need further warning of the serious consequences of failure to do so I can refer you to—'

The officer, tight-lipped, said in a thin voice:

'I should like to see your papers.'

Dawlish extracted his papers, and Ted did the same. The Home Guard officer examined the papers, stared past Dawlish towards the cars, and then said:

'I shall be compelled to detain you until inquiry has been made, Captain Dawlish.'

'Provided you detain the woman, that's all right with me,' said Dawlish. One man, a tall, gangling fellow in khaki denim overalls, opened his mouth.

'Mr. Moreton—'

'That's enough, Clarke.'

'Yes, sir, but—'

Moreton glared at him. 'Well, what is it?'

'Did you say Captain *Dawlish*, sir?'

'I did.'

'Well—I—strewth, don't you recognize him? Dawlish—you know, *Dawlish*. Had his photo in the papers.' He appealed to Dawlish. 'Isn't that right, Captain?'

Dawlish nodded.

'I hardly see how any press publicity you may have received affects the point at issue,' said Moreton. 'Understand, please, that you are under guard.'

'Right,' said Dawlish, amiably.

But he watched closely as Moreton walked to the Austin, a little afraid that the man might decide to be obstinate with a stubbornness encouraged rather than allayed by the verbal assault. Moreton, however, had changed his mind from his original decision; Lucille Lefroy was put into the rear of the Austin, and Felicity with her. The car was driven slowly back along the lane, being forced to go through a gap in the fence and for some yards across the fields in order to avoid the two wrecked cars. In a few minutes a two-seater was reached, and Moreton said abruptly.

'Drive with me, Captain Dawlish, please. Captain Beresford, will you get in the dicky seat?'

It was a small car, and Beresford was an outsize man, but he succeeded in squeezing his bulk into the seat. The car started at some speed towards a group of wooden buildings not far from the Great West Road. Outside a small door a sentry stood on guard with fixed bayonet.

They were admitted without question, since they were led by Moreton, and they entered a large room with sleeping bunks along one side, and a variety of indoor games filling up the rest of the accommodation. Four men in uniform were playing snooker, four others were gathered about a dart board. The tap-tap-tap of a ping-pong ball being smitten back and forth came from one end of the room.

As Beresford and Dawlish reached the players, a short, dark-haired fellow, bouncing like a bundle of india-rubber, smashed a winner.

'Oh, good shot!' exclaimed Beresford.

'Take you on for a tanner,' said the india-rubber man promptly, and Dawlish looked a little regretful.

'If I've time I'd be delighted.'

'You can stay here if you wish,' said Moreton unexpectedly. 'The inquiries will probably take half-an-hour. The woman will be well-cared for,' he added stiffly. She was, in fact, being carried through at that moment by two men. Felicity following them.

They were heading for a door marked First Aid. Moreton disappeared, while Dawlish entered into the game of ping-pong with some enthusiasm.

Suddenly Beresford began to chuckle.

Mystery—murder—confidential mission—a road chase—a trap—shooting—death and injury—and now *ping-pong!*

It was the india-rubber man's service, and he scored an ace.

'Eleven-three,' he said. 'Are you playing or aren't you? There's a tanner at stake, remember.'

'Oh, yes,' said Dawlish. 'A tanner. Right. Hide your grinning face Ted. I won't be able to concentrate if you don't.'

The india-rubber man served with ferocious attention.

Dawlish smashed a winner.

'Oh, good shot!' Every voice joined in that applause, and the attention grew even more wrapt. The india-rubber man flung himself into the game as if into battle, and a rally lasted for fifty seconds. Dawlish lost it, just missing the far edge of the table. There was another burst of applause. Beresford called:

'Fifteen-thirteen.'

At nineteen-all Moreton opened the door of his office, stared, stepped forward, but stopped whatever he was going to say and watched the speeding ball. Dawlish lost the point. A mutter of excitement went round the audience; if he lost the next he had lost the game. He took it with a lob that caught india-rubber by surprise.

'Twenty-all, best of five,' said that dark-haired little man.

'Best of five,' agreed Dawlish.

He lost two-three, and there was a terrific outburst of applause. He wiped his forehead, slipped his hand into his pocket and found a sixpence, sliding it along the table as the earlier loser had done with his pennies. The india-rubber man took it, and then gravely shook hands.

'A 'aven't 'ad a game like that since I come here,' he said. 'Play you double-or-quits, mister.'

'Done,' said Dawlish.

'Not just now, please,' said Moreton, and he looked at Dawlish with an unexpected smile on his lips. 'I've been in touch with the authorities, Captain Dawlish. I'm glad that you persuaded me to change my mind.'

Dawlish warmed to the District Commander.

'And I wish I hadn't let myself go so much,' he said. 'It mattered, and I was afraid you would insist.'

'If you'll come with me,' said Moreton, 'I'd like to make one or two notes for my report.'

They followed him into his bare office, and as the door closed behind them the guards in the big room burst into excited comment.

'Y-you don't get me,' one of them was saying. 'That's D-Dawlish. Don't you remember? S-Secret S-service and all that—'

'Don't be a twirp,' said the india-rubber man.

'Nobby's been reading another shocker,' someone else said.

'B-But it's true,' howled Nobby Clarke. 'What d'yer think that shooting was all about? W-hat—'

He stopped abruptly.

In Moreton's office the three men also turned their heads towards the door, for sharp and clear from outside came the report of a rifle shot. A shout followed—and then the sharper bark of an automatic, fired three times.

CHAPTER TWENTY-THREE

ONSLAUGHT

Dawlish reached the door first.

Inside the big room every man was standing staring towards the outside door. Another shout came, and then the door burst open—and there was a sharp gasp amongst the watchers. For the guard who entered had a bullet wound in his face—a glancing wound and one which bled so much that it looked worse than it was.

'We, we're being attacked!' he gasped.

He almost fell into the arms of the man nearest him, but before he spoke again Moreton's voice came, raised not in excitement or alarm, but crisp and reassuring.

'Get to your stations,' he said.

Men move quickly. One after another they picked rifles from the rack and went into the outer rooms, or through the main door, while from outside there was another burst of shooting.

Moreton looked sharply at Dawlish.

'This is connected with you, of course.'

'I'm just trying to believe it,' said Dawlish.

As he moved with Moreton towards the front door he realized what had happened. Others than the six men with the woman had been at hand, and they were staging an attack to get the prisoner back.

He had to accept it as a fact, and he knew that the importance of the woman was greater than he had realized.

He said tersely:

'How are you prepared, Moreton?'

'Fairly well, I think. We have sand-bagged posts in many directions, and men at them all. Unless there are fifty or sixty men outside I don't think there will be much danger.'

'Good,' said Dawlish. 'Can I have one of these—my ammunition's exhausted.' He picked a rifle out of the rack, and some ammunition from a box beside it. Beresford followed suit. When they reached the sand-bagged porch they saw that it was practically dark outside. Speckles of yellow were lighting the darkness in half-a-dozen places.

Dawlish said in a low voice:

'I'm going to get at the back of them. Is that all right?'

'If you really want to,' said Moreton, 'but there's no reason why you should put yourself in danger. My men will handle it. They'll be making an out-flanking movement now.' Moreton's eyes gleamed even in the poor light, and Dawlish guessed that the man was inwardly excited, pleased at a chance for a full-scale operation. The efficiency of the unit was a thing to marvel at.

A sharper burst of firing broke a short silence.

In the distance it was just possible to see cars passing along the road, although their lights were no more than pin-points. The shooting grew quicker.

Dawlish hesitated, a little uncertain.

He would have given a fortune to see how many men were

attacking, but even if he outflanked them that would not be easy, and he would be in danger from the fire of the guards as well as Bray's men. *Bray's men.* That was the fact at which his mind jibbed; that they had *dared*, to stage an attack like this was almost incredible.

How big *was* the organization?

He played again with the idea of making a sortie, but he was fully convinced of the efficiency of the guards, and he wanted to do nothing to prevent them enjoying what Moreton clearly believed would be a triumph.

Moreton said quietly:

'Leave it to them, Captain Dawlish.'

'Ri-ight,' said Dawlish.

It was odd to stand there, behind a stout pile of sandbags, and to hear the fighting, yet to take no part in it. He did not know how long he waited.

And then suddenly the shooting grew faster.

It grew, in fact, into a veritable volley. Voices were added to the barking of shots, and then there was a rush of footsteps. Moreton exclaimed:

'They've got them!'

Dawlish, Beresford and Moreton moved forward, footsteps thudded, the sound of heavy breathing, of steel against steel, of sharp oaths, rent the night. Then suddenly another shot, and a louder report—the bursting of a tyre.

An engine roared.

By then Dawlish's eyes were more accustomed to the gloom and, perhaps fifty yards away, he saw the outline of a car. He believed at first that three men were in it, but as the engine awakened to life and the car began to move a little, other figures materialized. Confused sounds followed, and then the engine was cut out abruptly.

Silence followed.

A figure appeared, and saluted Moreton.

'Seven prisoners for interrogation, sir.'

Then followed a procession of men, each prisoner unarmed and with an escort. Three men were carried—one of the three, Dawlish noticed with a sharp pang of regret, was in Home Guard uniform.

Beresford drew a deep, wondering breath.

'Would you have believed it?'

'Not in a thousand years,' said Dawlish, 'although I should have done. So should you, for that matter. Moreton's got them lined up as good as, or a damned sight better, than the active army.' They retraced their steps to the main building.

Moreton was looking over the seven prisoners.

Dawlish could see nothing exceptional about them, unless it was in the uniformity of their clothes—they all wore dark grey. For the rest they were middle-aged men, who might have been found in any gathering. Most were not only well-dressed, but had the appearance of well-bred men.

At Moreton's request Dawlish joined that remarkable man in his office. There was no doubt that he was pleased beyond measure, and he prefaced his remarks with a wide smile.

'When I saw you first, Dawlish, I didn't think I'd be thanking you before the night was out. This will put our fellows on top of the world—and they've worked damned hard! They'll deserve everything they get. Well now—you'll want to interrogate the prisoners, I suppose?'

Dawlish smiled.

'I don't see why you shouldn't do that—but I do appreciate your change of front. Inquiries about me were fairly satisfactory I gather.'

Moreton smiled. 'Much more than that. A Chief Inspector Trivett also told me that you were acting with special authority, and that is good enough for me.'

'Thanks,' said Dawlish. 'And quite seriously—apologies for that rudery of mine. But I was as anxious to keep the woman as her friends were to get her—you've judged what inspired the attack I take it?'

'Oh, of course. And if I'd sent her to the hospital under a small guard they would have got her all right. We'll forget that little difference, shall we?' Moreton looked eagerly towards the door with the hopeful enthusiasm of a subaltern facing the prospect of his first inquiry. 'If you're really serious about me questioning those men, I'd better get busy. I'd rather get some information before I send in any report.'

'You go ahead,' said Dawlish. 'I'm going to Town,' he added, 'with the lady prisoner, I'm quite sure the others will be all right with you here. Keep them under close guard, and don't have them sent anywhere else until Beresford or I come back. If the police raise any query, refer them to Scotland Yard.'

'Excellent!' said Moreton crisply. 'I'll do that.'

The Home Guard had brought Beresford's Talbot from the lane, and now Dawlish, Beresford, Felicity and the prisoner were bundled into it.

None of them talked much on the way to London, and as they reached the centre of the city the air-raid alert whined and moaned about them for the first time since Dawlish and Beresford had reached King's Cross. Soon afterwards the first reports of ack-ack fire echoed not far away.

Beresford looked over his shoulder.

'Where are we going, Pat?'

'Montgomery's office,' said Dawlish.

They knocked at the side door, and were admitted by a

servant whom Dawlish had seen at this earlier visit to the flat above the salon.

Beresford carried the woman upstairs, and Dawlish and Felicity followed them. Felicity was on edge, although she hardly knew why. She had been composed enough in the fighting, but now that they were at Montgomery's headquarters she was inwardly perturbed.

If Montgomery felt surprise at seeing Beresford calmly carrying an unconscious woman into the room he did not show it. He was accompanied by a tall, dark-haired man whom Dawlish had seen at King's Cross and who had actually travelled with Julia Dawnay. Both men appeared to be worried.

'What *is* this?' Montgomery demanded a little petulantly.

'A prisoner of importance, I hope,' Dawlish explained. He very much wanted to know what had upset the two men.

Montgomery licked his lips.

'Dawlish, I have just had a message from Julia Dawnay. She has been hurt—not badly, but enough to put her out of action for a day or two. I—er—'

He hesitated, and then looked squarely into Dawlish's eyes; but Dawlish, Beresford and Felicity were thinking only of one thing—of Tim Jeremy, and what had happened to him.

Montgomery's hesitation seemed to imply disaster for Tim.

CHAPTER TWENTY-FOUR

MISSING MEMBER

'Go on,' said Dawlish gruffly.

Beresford put his burden down in an easy chair. She moved her head a little, the first small sign of returning consciousness—but none of them saw it. They had eyes only for Montgomery and the man with him, ears only for the news Montgomery could give.

'I can't give you much information,' Montgomery said at last. 'There was a car smash, and Miss Dawnay was able to crawl away unobserved. The car was surrounded by men, and she believes that Jeremy was taken from the wreckage. She can't be sure.'

'Oh,' said Dawlish.

He lit a cigarette, his hands a little unsteady. 'We'll get word soon, I suppose.' He spoke in a harsh voice, and there seemed no emotion in him. 'Now for my report, Colonel. This woman is in a position to give us considerable information—vital information.'

Montgomery looked at Lucille. He was silent for some seconds, and then he pulled himself together, grew more brisk and formal.

'Just what happened?' he asked.

Dawlish explained briefly.

'Very well done, Dawlish—I'm certainly glad we came to an arrangement. Have you interrogated her?'

'Not yet,' said Dawlish. 'And she hasn't been searched. Felicity, will you do that? We can go out for a few minutes, but,' he added for the woman's benefit, 'we'll leave the door ajar.' He looked at Montgomery for agreement, and the Colonel nodded. The four men filed into a small ante-room, and Montgomery said a little abruptly:

'Captain Dawlish—this is Mr. Forbes. My second-in-command.'

'How do 'you do?' Forbes murmured.

Dawlish looked briefly at the good-looking face, the natty, well-cut suit. He disliked the man on sight; and had done so from the first glance. He had an uneasy feeling that the dark eyes concealed more than they revealed.

'And Captain Beresford,' said Montgomery.

'I am really delighted, gentlemen,' said Forbes.

Beresford thought: 'Pat says there's a leakage in high places. I wonder . . .'

'Really delighted,' continued Forbes. 'My activities of late have been a little uncertain—I often envy gentlemen like yourselves, so direct, so concerned with action.' He smiled. 'You are to be warmly congratulated on the results you have achieved.'

There was a slight, rather awkward pause.

Montgomery cleared his throat.

Dawlish said abruptly: 'About this woman, Colonel Montgomery—she is not likely to prove talkative—'

'It's rather early to say that,' interrupted Forbes.

Dawlish looked at him coolly.

'I don't think so. My experience of her leads me to suppose she will not respond to orthodox methods.'

'Precisely what do you mean?' asked Forbes.

Dawlish's smile was both formal and cold, but what answer he was likely to give was cut short by Felicity's call that she had finished the search.

They went into the room, to find the woman sitting up, not only fully conscious but very well aware of what was going on around her. Dawish wondered a little testily whether he should have brought her here, or taken her to the flat. He had an unpleasant conviction that Forbes would object to even the mildest form of third degree.

Felicity had laid a small pile of oddments on the corner of Montgomery's desk. The hand bag was there, with the lining turned inside out, a powder compact, lipstick, some notes, amounting in all to about eleven pounds, a small pile of silver, a note-book, a comb and mirror, a diamond ring—for some reason Dawlish was surprised by that—and a small pile of visiting cards.

There were no letters and no other papers.

He picked up one of the cards, and saw that it had been printed on the same machine as the card which Sebastian Bray had given him. It read:

Lucille Lefroy.

He looked into her amber eyes bleakly.

'So it's Lucille, is it?'

She said nothing; he was not to know that she was deciding that Fesell had been quite wrong in one respect: here was no blundering fool who could not use his head. But Fesell had been right on another count; Dawlish was dangerous.

'Tongue-tied, are you?' said Dawlish roughly. 'And you don't put your address on your visiting card. Odd. Or isn't it?' He turned the card over, and said in an even voice, 'Where do you live?'

She did not speak.

'I said—'

'Captain Dawlish. I wonder if I can interrupt,' asked Forbes, suavely. He did not say so, but his manner suggested that here was the need for a little tact, and he did not believe that Dawlish could employ it. 'Miss Lefroy, you are doing yourself no service by remaining obdurate. Your address, please.'

Lucille turned the full stare of her amber eyes on him, and spoke for the first time. As her lips opened there was a smile of anticipatory triumph on Forbes's face.

She said gently:

'Do you want to come to see me?'

Forbes coloured, and Montgomery snapped:

'That attitude won't help you—'

'Now, let's get this quite straight,' said Lucille, and she spoke with an American accent which would convince most—but not Dawlish. 'I'm not speaking to you, or to anyone. I demand to see my Consul.'

'This is not the time for endeavouring to use any privilege,' said Montgomery sharply. 'Are you an American?'

'What did you think I was—a Turk?'

Beresford glanced at Dawlish, and for the first time since the news of Timothy's disaster there was a smile in Dawlish's eyes. He did not think that either Montgomery or Forbes were going to have a good time with Lucille Lefroy. He was quite sure by then that he should have taken the woman to the flat.

'By asking for a consul you have admitted you are an alien,' said Montgomery sharply. 'You have acted in a manner which—'

'For Pete's sake!' exclaimed Dawlish. 'If I'm not crazy now, I'm being driven that way! I think we should take the prisoner to a police station, sir.'

'It is not a police matter,' objected Montgomery.

'It can be made one,' said Dawlish sharply.

'I really think that we can handle the matter here more efficaciously than elsewhere,' interposed Forbes. 'I am quite sure that Miss Lefroy will quickly realize the uselessness of her attitude.'

Dawlish said woodenly: 'You haven't the facilities here for keeping her prisoner. Or have you?'

Montgomery looked doubtful.

'Good,' said Dawlish briskly. 'I telephoned Canon Row before I came here, and told them to expect her. We'll take her now, I think.' His hand closed round Lucille's arm.

'I will accompany you,' said Forbes quietly.

'No need,' said Dawlish.

'I want you here,' said Montgomery quietly. Dawlish breathed a sigh of relief as he walked downstairs with Lucille, gripping her arm firmly. He would not have been surprised had she made an effort to dodge away in the black-out, but she did no such thing.

'Where to?' asked Beresford.

'The flat,' said Dawlish.

He felt the woman's arm stiffen, but she made no comment as she was hustled into the car. They reached Jermyn Street in a little more than five minutes, and Felicity opened the door with a key.

They went into the small hallway.

And then they stopped in the darkness, for beneath a door opposite them there was a thin line of light.

'Well, well, well!' Dawlish murmured under his breath, 'visitors, and foolish enough to leave the light on. Watch her, Ted.'

He released Lucille, and stepped slowly to the door, treading softly.

He had his automatic—empty but good enough for show purposes—when he turned the handle and threw open the door. He saw a woman standing by the fireplace. It was Julia, and in her hand, pointing straight at his heart, was an automatic.

CHAPTER TWENTY-FIVE

OBSTINATE LADY

Dawlish looked steadily at the small automatic.

He heard Felicity catch her breath, and heard a rumble in Ted's throat, but the moment of tension eased quickly, as Julia lowered the gun.

'You had me scared that time,' she said.

Dawlish pushed his hand through his hair.

'That goes for all of us, I fancy. Who did you think it was?'

'I don't know. I was ready for anyone. Thank heavens you're safe,' she added. 'Who is that?'

'The name is Lucille—Lucille Lefroy. Does it mean anything?'

Julia shook her head.

'Pity,' said Dawlish, 'although I suppose we can't expect too much in a single day.' He watched Ted lead Lucille to a chair, and her graceful sinking into it. It reminded him very forcibly of a film seductress. But for the thought of Tim he would have been really amused.

'What happened to you?' he asked.

Julia said in a low voice.

'The cab followed us as far as Basingstoke—'

'By George, you went far enough!'

'Tim insisted,' said Julia. 'Then we met another car, coming towards us. There wasn't a lot of traffic about, and at first I thought it was an accident. I soon learned differently. They forced us into a ditch. Tim was caught by the steering wheel. I was flung clear.'

'Yes?' said Dawlish bleakly.

'I had to get away,' said Julia. 'I hated to leave him, but—there were half-a-dozen of them. They started searching. I wandered about a bit and then I almost fell against a sentry guarding a small camp. I managed to persuade them to look for Tim and the men, but they had all gone before the search started.'

Dawlish rubbed his chin slowly.

'Too bad. We've had quite an official night,' His voice grew tense. 'Was—Tim in the wreckage?'

'No. There was no one there.'

'Thank the Lord for that!' exclaimed Beresford. 'They wouldn't have troubled to move him had he been dead.' He brought the last word out with a considerable effort. Dawlish nodded.

'That's an argument, at all events. Montgomery thought you were more badly hurt than you are,' he added to Julia.

Julia said slowly:

'I meant him to.'

Her eyes matched Dawlish's: he knew that she wanted to enlarge on what she had said, but would not do so while Lucille was there. He walked with Julia into the next room.

She turned impulsively to him:

'Pat, it's crazy I know, but I'm beginning to hate Montgomery. He's hedging everything with ifs and buts and conditions. I— oh, I know that I'm looking at the personal angle more than I should, but taking orders from him just lead nowhere. I've never known a man change as much.'

Dawlish smiled.

'Our Colonel is a worried man,' he said. 'Someone's got to be the scapegoat for the St. John murder, you know. Montgomery really had charge of it.'

'Do you think that's on his mind?'

'I certainly do,' said Dawlish. 'Now, before we go in there, I want to know more about Forbes. Did he work for your father?'

'No. He was posted a month ago from the Foreign Office.'

'Oh, ho,' said Dawlish. 'A real live diplomat. How does he impress you?'

'He's clever,' said Julia. 'I don't like him, but like or dislike doesn't count.' She brushed a hand across her eyes.

They rejoined the others.

Lucille looked up at Dawlish with more than a touch of insolence and contempt.

'What have you worked out?' she demanded in the nasal tones that had so little connection with her normal speaking voice.

Dawlish said easily:

'Nothing for you yet, my pet. You will keep for a little while. On the whole, I'm not complaining. Three dead, eight prisoners, and you. Quite coming into the open, aren't you?'

Her eyes narrowed.

'What are you saying?'

Dawlish sat on the edge of a chair and contemplated her.

'Why don't you stop pretending to be an American?' he demanded. 'It isn't convincing.'

'I'm not pretending—'

'Listen, beautiful,' said Dawlish, and he leaned closer towards her. 'When you first opened those sweet lips of yours you spoke English as if you'd never been out of the country. Remember?'

There was a moment of silence, and then slowly Lucille smiled. When she spoke it was in her normal voice.

'You don't miss much, do you?'

'I hope not. This isn't the time for missing things. Do you know why Montgomery let me take you away?'

'Tell me,' she said.

'Because he knows he must get results quickly, and knew that he wouldn't be able to persuade you to talk. He has a greater faith in me.'

She looked at him without fear.

'Large men are reputed to be soft-hearted,' he went on. 'Here's one that isn't. Too many men have been killed, too many things are at stake. I want a story from you, and a true one. If necessary I'll force it out of you, and I mean force. You've got half-an-hour to think it over. Think hard, and above all, think fast.' He turned away from her. 'Well, folk,' he said, 'we had better freshen ourselves up while we're waiting.' He picked up the telephone. He would have had difficulty with a private call, but was connected with Scotland Yard at once. Now and again the cracking of anti-aircraft batteries sounded unpleasantly close, and once or twice the drone of enemy planes could be heard overhead: but it was doubtful if anyone in that room realized the nearness of danger.

Dawlish said: 'Inspector Trivett, please . . . all right, Detective Sergeant Munk . . . well, is Sir Archibald Morely in?'

'Who is that speaking, please?'

'Captain Dawlish,' said Dawlish, and a few seconds afterwards he was speaking to Morely.

'Urgent and important inquiry about to be put in hand,' he said with a smile, as if Morely could see him. 'There's a woman named Lefroy—Lucille Lefroy. You may or may not have her on your records, but she's the type who would probably be well known wherever she lives. Will you put out a call for any information about her.'

'Primarily what?' asked Morely.

'Her address,' said Dawlish. 'She may not be using her right name, of course, and if she isn't we haven't a lot of chance, but here's a description: five-foot eight, full-figure—weighs about ten-and-a-half stone, I'd say—fair hair, amber eyes.'

'What colour eyes?' asked Morely.

'You're right, it's not usual,' said Dawlish. 'Amber. As per the second light on traffic signals, and nearly as deceiving I fancy.' He smiled into the telephone. 'I can't help thinking I've seen her, or someone very like her before.'

There was a pause before Morely said crisply:

'All right, I'll see what I can find out.'

'And while you're doing it,' went on Dawlish, 'you might send a shorthand typist over—I'd like to dictate a statement. Good man. Oh, and I say, what about those four permits?'

'They're on the way to you,' said Morely, and he rang down.

The talk seemed to have done Dawlish good. He went back a little on his heels, and hummed *So Deep is the Night* in a baritone that was not unpleasant, although he missed on several notes.

'We proceed,' he said. 'I don't know what Morely will make of that lot.'

He looked at Lucille, a speculative gleam in his eye. He had until that moment averted his gaze from her; a quick glance had told him, however, that she was feeling the strain, and was nothing like as confident as she had been ten minutes before. She was not trying to smile, and her eyes were very hard, and narrowed—she looked at him all the time.

He continued to look at her, and said to Ted:

'Ted, is your flat empty?'

'My flat?' Beresford just saved himself from sounding surprised. 'Well, it's a bit blackened and charred, you know.'

'Hmm. But I think you'd better get the girls there,' said

Dawlish. 'They won't want to stay.' He looked fleetingly at Felicity. 'It's a pity, darling, but Lovely Lucille doesn't look as if she's thinking hard enough, and there will have to be persuasion. On the other hand, it may be as well.' His eyes were not smiling or mocking as he regarded the prisoner again; they were very hard and cold.

She spoke suddenly, even unexpectedly.

'Dawlish, what were you saying about having seen me before?'

Dawlish looked surprised.

'Saying? Oh, about you, yes. There is a faint similarity between you and a man I once knew—about the eyes. Interested?'

She stared at him.

Her lips had tightened, so that they looked much thinner than they were. Her manner riveted their attention, even Dawlish's: and so did her words.

'So it was you who killed him!'

CHAPTER TWENTY-SIX

REQUEST FROM LUCILLE

Very slowly and deliberately Dawlish took his cigarette-case from his pocket. He squashed out the stub of the cigarette he was smoking, but before he put another to his lips he proffered the case to Lucille. After a moment's hesitation she accepted. He lit up for himself and for her, watching the thin spirals of smoke.

'Killed whom?' he said.

'You know damned well who I mean.'

'No,' said Dawlish, 'you're wrong. The eyes were the same though. Relationship seemed indicated.'

'He was my brother,' she said.

Just two spots of red burned on her cheeks; the pallor of the rest of her face was startling, making Beresford, Julia and Felicity stare at her rather than at Dawlish.

He said slowly: 'I see. However, you're wrong. I didn't kill him.'

'I don't believe you.'

Dawlish shrugged his shoulders.

'Please yourself. I'm not much interested in any case. He might have been useful had he lived, but he didn't regain consciousness before they blew him up.'

'They did *what*?'

Carefully Dawlish tapped the ash from his cigarette.

'Blew him up. But I needn't confuse you over the details. I first saw him in my flat after I had differed from your friend Bray. He was unconscious—your brother I mean. The flat was on fire. He was drugged. Had I been ten minutes later he would have died. He—'

'Pat,' said Ted Beresford in a strained voice, 'was that poor beggar at the flat her brother?'

'So she says; he had her eyes, anyhow. Where was I? Oh, yes, he was drugged and I carried him out of danger. It looked to me like an attempt to frame me with a drugging-cum-murder-by-fire charge, but it wasn't that altogether. You see, I sent for a police ambulance. He was loaded in it. A gentleman on a motor-cycle threw a bomb.' Although he spoke in unfamiliar short sentences, his words and his manner were compelling and perhaps the more convincing. 'Quite clearly they needed to kill him, and having failed one way they succeeded in another. For what comfort I can give you, he was unconscious when he died, which is more than can be said of the ambulance attendants with him. On the whole, I do not like your friends.'

There was a long moment of silence, and then unexpectedly Lucille licked her lips. It was an odd gesture; it suggested to Dawlish—as well as to Felicity—that she was not quite sure of herself. More: Dawlish imagined that she was trying not to believe what he had told her.

Dawlish had never been one to ignore odd chances.

Many of the apparently inconsequential things he did and said were deliberate, attempts to get information, to test the reaction of this man or that in certain circumstances; he had seen the likeness of the eyes and assumed a relationship, and he had used his theory to the fullest advantage. Now the woman was looking at him fixedly and yet uncertain in herself. The coolness—not bravado, but the genuine coolness of a woman not easily frightened—had gone.

Dawlish would not have been surprised had she said: 'I don't believe you' even though she might have said it unconvincingly. But she did nothing of the kind.

'When was this?' she asked.

'Last evening,' said Dawlish. 'Bray came to see me, talked wildly, and was unfortunate enough to get knocked about a little. He got away when I wasn't looking. During that time your brother was taken to the flat and the flat was fired. I hope,' he added quietly, 'that Bray doesn't make a habit of acting against instructions.'

Again she licked her lips.

'If Bray did that—' she began, and then she stopped. She seemed to take a greater hold on herself, and said sharply: 'Where is Bray?'

It caused a sensation.

True, none of the four people listening showed that. Dawlish did not even alter his expression. Beresford's face went suddenly tense. Felicity stopped in the middle of a breath and then went on. Julia moved a little in the chair she had taken. But the silence lasted even longer than the previous one, and when Dawlish at last broke it his manner was not unlike Lucille's had been—as if he did not want to believe what he had heard.

'Don't you know?' he demanded.

She drew a deep breath.

'No. I only knew that he had failed in his job.'

'My fault, I'm afraid,' said Dawlish.

'I can believe it,' said Lucille, and for the first time since the talk of her brother's death something like a smile crossed her face. 'A great many things are your fault, Dawlish. Will you strike a bargain with me?'

'I'll consider it.'

'Yes, or no?'

'Nothing arranged in advance,' said Dawlish gently. 'But if you offer me anything that might be of value I'll consider an exchange of information.'

Again she stared at him fixedly, and then she put the cigarette to her lips; it had gone out, and Dawlish flicked his lighter into flame, and leaned forward. She drew in the smoke hungrily.

'Dawlish, exactly what *is* your part in this business?'

Dawlish pursed his lips.

'Very nearly *ex-officio*,' he said. 'Object, to stop the dirty work. Obviously Bray wasn't what he was supposed to be, and I managed to make that clear. However, the death of an Eire envoy made things considerably more difficult. I want the killer. I'll even say,' he added slowly, 'that I'll get the killer. But that's a result, not a cause. I want to break the organization that you and Bray decorate so diversely. Got that?'

'Ye-es.' Her eyes were very narrow: cat's eyes, thought Dawlish. 'Ye-es,' she repeated. 'There's nothing personal in it?'

'There is not.'

'You're a peculiar man,' she said, 'but I suppose you know that. I don't give a damn what you do with Bray,' she added, 'or what you have done with him. He fell down on his job. He is no longer any use to us. If I were sure that it was he who arranged to kill Toby—'

Into the following pause Dawlish said:

'Toby was your brother?'

'Yes. You might understand him, Dawlish, although I never could. I'm not interested in who rules in Ireland. Toby was—'

From Beresford came a gentle exclamation.

'I.R.A., is it?'

'Yes,' said Lucille stonily. 'He was a fanatic for the I.R.A. That's why he helped us. He *believed* what he fought for—can you understand that, Dawlish?'

'I can,' said the large man soberly.

'He didn't know what was happening,' Lucille added almost dreamily. 'I think he would have killed me had he known. But he didn't know!' she added more sharply. 'He couldn't know!'

Dawlish said: 'We're not in full agreement.'

She looked at him as if afraid of what he was going to say.

'I think he did know,' Dawlish said. 'It would explain so much, your brother was a patriot, a fanatic—right or wrong doesn't matter, he fought for an ideal. He discovered Bray was racketeering: he grew dangerous, and therefore had to be killed. Doesn't it speak for itself?' he asked gently.

She turned her face away abruptly, and began to pace the room with short, agitated steps. To the others it was as if the façade of hardness and of crime, of intrigue and of murder, had been torn away by the personal issue, by that queer blood-bondage which revealed itself in so many unexpected ways.

'It can't be true,' she said, but clearly she thought that it was. 'Bray would have told me—'

'Bray didn't have a lot of time to work in,' Dawlish said. 'Things moved a little too quickly for him. And I.R.A. men aren't known for their discretion. If he thought he had been tricked he would have sworn vengeance and tried to get it there and then.'

It was odd that a dead man, a man, moreover, who had apparently been used to try to incriminate Dawlish, should have such influence.

Dawlish and the others knew that it was in this woman's power to lead them to their goal. She would not easily be persuaded; Dawlish doubted whether any measure of third degree would be effective, and he would certainly fall short of the lengths to which experts at the art would go. And Dawlish knew that in the dead Toby Lefroy there was a power greater than he possessed, a power to make her talk.

Would it succeed?

As if unaware that anyone was in the room with her, Lucille said softly:

'Bray would do it, if he thought it necessary, but would he tell Lia first? Would *Lia* do it?' To Dawlish the name she used sounded like 'Leah' and he wondered whether another woman could be in this affair, whether the direction genius was feminine. None of them moved or spoke, until Lucille went on: 'We should never have used Bray; Toby was always against it.'

Dawlish dared to ask: 'Why?'

She looked at him, suddenly startled, and then she went on in the same casual, detached tone:

'Bray was a member of the old I.R.A. party. Then he went to America, played a large part in some of the rackets there, and then returned to Ireland and set himself up as a political boss. Didn't you know?'

'Not all of it,' said Dawlish.

'You haven't been told much,' she said. 'He was rich—and there aren't many really rich men in Ireland. I suppose you knew *that.*' There was a sardonic twist in her smile as she looked at him, and he was a little afraid that she had recovered from the shock of learning how her brother had been killed. But she went on talking, giving him information, only part of which he could have learned from Trivett.

'He had English contacts, and he bought up most of the electrical companies in Ireland. It wasn't known that he had them— he "cornered" them in the best American fashion—and—Lia helped him. Don't ask who Lia is,' she said; 'in any case, you wouldn't know him.'

'Him,' thought Dawlish, and in a measure he was relieved.

'Bray was smart,' she went on, 'but he could never hold himself down. Then, when this envoy was needed for England, he showed part of his hand. He had this corner in Eire utilities. Dublin had to listen to him. He impressed them with his commercial contacts in England—he told them that he could exert his influence to get a good deal. Dublin needed bullion—'

She stopped abruptly.

For a moment no one spoke, but four pairs of eyes were directed towards her, Dawlish's narrowed and hard, the others wide in surprise—the surprise that she had given them through talking just that little bit too much. It was useless for her to pretend she had not mentioned the word, or to hope that the casual mention meant nothing to them. She had made her first major mistake; all of them were aware of it.

'Go on,' said Dawlish gently.

'You're good at guessing, aren't you?' she said, and there was a sardonic inflection in her voice. 'Well, you won't take long to guess that one. All right, Dawlish, I'll assume you guess right. That's the key—bullion, red gold—a million pounds of it. Ireland wants a million as the first payment against goods, not in credit but in gold—she's got little or no reserve. Well, other people can use a million in gold, Dawlish.'

'Ye-es,' said Dawlish in a strained voice.

So much was clear, then.

Bray, with influence on both sides of the Irish Sea, enough to get him a hearing, negotiating for the Trade Treaty and the million pounds in bullion—Bray knowing how and when it was to be shipped, *and Bray in a position to have it sent astray once it reached Eire*. A prize worth any man's biggest effort if the man had the twisted mentality which would make him go for it at all.

And a careless word had told Dawlish.

How much more could he learn?

There was much more at stake of course—complications it was almost impossible to unravel then and there, but as his eyes matched the woman's he thought of her offer of a 'bargain' and he wondered whether he dared go on with it.

CHAPTER TWENTY-SEVEN

DAWLISH STRIKES A BARGAIN

Dawlish said quietly and with more control over his voice than he had expected to have:

'So that's the way it goes? Bray was to arrange for this bullion shipment, and then to hand it over to you and your Lia. Not bad,' he agreed judiciously. 'A pity Bray's failed. But you've given yourself time to put someone else up to Dublin as the negotiator-in-chief by killing St. John, haven't you? I feel badly about that.'

She did not try to evade the fact.

'Yes, St. John had to go,' she said. 'He went all right—'

'*Via* Bray.'

Lucille smiled sardonically. 'Oh no. Bray didn't have anything to do with St. John's murder. That was arranged my end.'

'The feminine touch,' Dawlish murmured.

'Don't start getting fresh with words,' Lucille said roughly. 'You know I don't give a damn for who dies or who lives—'

'With one exception,' Dawlish murmured.

'I'm not going to start getting sentimental about Toby now,' she rasped. 'I'll get Bray for it, the swine, but—' she paused. 'Let us understand each other, Dawlish. I'm in this business.'

'Up to your pretty neck,' agreed Dawlish.

'I'll look after my neck,' she flashed. 'I wanted to get you, and your friends, but it didn't succeed. When it failed and you caught me, my neck was in all the danger it could be, and anything I tell you about killing St. John won't make any difference.'

'That's honest,' admitted Dawlish.

'I'm not wasting time now on anything that isn't a fact,' Lucille said. 'But I've got knowledge you want, Dawlish—I'm not going to let it go while I'm in danger.'

'Ah,' said Dawlish. 'Your life for your information, is that it?'

'Not quite,' she said.

'I'm at least listening,' said Dawlish. 'And by the way, could you drink coffee? Or tea? Or even—'

'Oh, something stronger, much stronger,' she said.

Dawlish made an airy movement towards the cocktail bar and glasses, while Ted opened a couple of bottles. None of them wasted time in elaborate approach, but drank quickly.

'Thanks,' Lucille said. 'Well, Dawlish, you know the situation now.'

'Ye-es,' admitted Dawlish. 'I also know that the gold bullion won't be shipped, whoever makes the arrangements. That little scheme has had it's *quietus*, at least until you and your friends are no longer at large. You've gathered that?'

She smiled thinly.

'You'll try to stop it, but you mustn't be too sure that the politicians will believe you.'

'A point,' admitted Dawlish. 'Y'know, Lucille, we could have much in common.'

'Well, we haven't. Dawlish, I want to go from here, quite free. I—'

'Remarkable!' said Dawlish.

'Don't joke!' she snapped. 'You can stop me, of course, I can be in jail tonight and in the dock tomorrow, and hanged in two months' time—all right, I know it. But I want to go for more reasons than my safety. I want to find out who else knew about Toby. If—if Lia did, I'll come back to you, and give you all the information you want.'

Ted Beresford stopped in the middle of a drink.

'Well, well,' he said, 'you do think we're simple.'

'Doesn't she?' asked Dawlish, but although he smiled he did not seem wholly amused. 'Who is this Lia?'

'He controls the arrangements.'

'Your gunmen, Bray, and all?' asked Dawlish.

'Yes, all of it.'

'Quite a personage,' said Dawlish. 'What is he to you?'

'We've been around together for a long time.'

'Love and all that?' asked Dawlish.

'You don't say "love" and "Lia" in the same breath,' she told him, and he knew then that whatever relationship she had with the unknown Lia, from her point of view it was one which was carefully and coldly considered.

'Well, what then?' he said.

'If Lia knew about Toby, I'll come back.'

'Just that?' He raised his eyebrows.

'If I come I'll talk,' she said, 'I'll tell you everything I know against my freedom, Dawlish. I'd agree to go abroad, to anywhere you name.'

'I see,' said Dawlish. 'And if Lia didn't know about Toby?'

'That would be your bad luck,' said Lucille.

Again there was silence, and it was Beresford who broke it. Throughout the interview Julia and Felicity had said nothing, but there was little they had missed. And they knew as well as

Dawlish that he would have to make a decision quickly; nor did Felicity doubt what the decision would be.

'Thing is,' Beresford said judiciously, 'if we take her at her word, Pat, that's a big enough gamble. But this chap might lie to her—almost certainly will do, under the circumstances. So we stand to lose both ways.'

Dawlish nodded.

'If he had anything to do with it,' said Lucille evenly, 'I'll find out. Don't worry about that.'

Julia broke in, speaking for the first time. There was tension in her voice, and her eyes were very bright.

'Pat, you can't be sure she's telling the truth. It's simply a desperate ruse to get away.'

Dawlish turned to Lucille. 'You've set us quite a problem, Beautiful. The trouble is, we don't trust you.'

Lucille shrugged. 'You either take that chance, or you don't.'

The odd thing to Dawlish was that she did not seem to mind. He had been thinking swiftly, and he reasoned that the men who had been with her when they had tried to take him a prisoner had taken instructions from someone else—probably Lia—before making their desperate effort to get her free.

Why had Lia—if it had been he—shown such concern?

Clearly, Dawlish reasoned, because he knew that she could give too much away.

He spoke suddenly and sharply.

'Let's get this straight. You'll go to Lia, and if he had any part in your brother's murder you'll double-cross him in exchange for your own safety. Is that it?'

The girl nodded.

'Supposing we get your information and don't let you go free?'

'That will be my gamble,' she said.

'Ye-es,' said Dawlish. 'What other conditions?'

'That you don't try to follow me.'

'Pat,' said Julia tensely, 'she's lying her way out of here.'

'It's possible,' admitted Dawlish, 'but it isn't certain, Julia, and in this business we have to take some chances. However, there are not quite as much odds against us as it might seem. If I let you go,' he said to Lucille in a sharper voice, 'I won't have you followed, but I won't stop trying to locate you by other means.'

'What other means?'

'Oh, no,' said Dawlish. 'That's my affair. After all, we're being honest.'

She returned his gaze evenly.

'Yes, we're being honest,' she said. 'Well—do you agree?'

'Subject to one condition,' Dawlish said.

Her breast was rising and falling quickly, as if she knew that everything depended on the nature of his condition. Felicity, Julia and Beresford watched in silence; Julia looked likely to break into protestations at any moment.

'Go on,' said Lucille.

'I want to know just what has inspired you against me,' said Dawlish, 'and how you learned that I was likely to be interested, why you made such desperate efforts to get me, and what has happened to Jeremy.'

She stared at him for some seconds, and he saw that her hands were clenched very tightly.

'I can't tell you all. Bray worked quite a lot off his own bat. We haven't heard from him since yesterday morning; for all we know he might be dead. Abel—the cabby—will take Jeremy to Lia. There were several cars of men waiting nearby for you.'

'Who were the men?'

She laughed at him, an unexpected thing.

'Haven't you guessed that?'

Dawlish said very gently: 'I suppose I have. Toby wasn't the only I.R.A. patriot you used, was he?'

'Lia makes use of them, yes. They believe in him, thinking his interest is theirs.'

That also explained a great deal.

It told Dawlish, amongst other things, why the men had been ready to attack a Home Guard unit, and why they were prepared to risk their lives so recklessly. They believed that in so doing they were promoting the cause of Ireland, and he knew that such men would scorn any thought of personal safety in the execution of what they considered to be their life's mission.

More; it suggested that none of them would be easily persuaded to talk.

He said slowly: 'All right, go on.'

'Lia told me, and told Bray, you were coming down,' she said. 'Lia had a dossier of all men who might be used against us. He knew what you had done in the past and he warned Bray. He told him your weakest spot was for your girl—' she turned her eyes for a moment towards Felicity, as if trying to understand why that should be, but she did not stop talking in the swift, almost urgent voice with which she had started. 'Bray was told he would have to stop you—I don't know how or why he failed. Abel merely told us the house had been blown up and that he had got most of the men away before this happened. Abel would be in charge after Bray.'

'Would Abel have authority to destroy the house himself?'

'In emergency, yes.'

'Did he say anything about Bray?'

'No—I haven't seen him. He telephoned Lia.'

'I see,' said Dawlish gently. 'And then?'

'We started on you. I had arranged to contact Abel and two cars of men near Jermyn Street. He would arrange to stop Jeremy, and whoever was with him.'

'Ye-es,' said Dawlish. 'Another thing. What was in the St. John's Wood house?'

'Records,' she said simply.

'Of what?'

'The I.R.A. organization in this country. There are duplicates,' she added, and again there was a sardonic tone in her voice: 'you haven't destroyed *them*. Lia uses the organization,' she added. 'He managed that through Bray—Bray had them eating out of his hand—or he used to have.'

Dawlish nodded.

'All right, Lucille, I'm taking a chance on you. You're as free as the air.'

The door closed behind her with a snap, and as she disappeared Julia rushed towards Dawlish and gripped his wrist. Her fingers bit into the flesh, with a pressure which told him something of the nervous tension which possessed her.

'You must follow her!' she said urgently, 'you mustn't let her go!'

Dawlish said gently: 'I have made a bargain.'

'How can you be such a fool?' Julia demanded passionately. 'She was lying her way out, I tell you. You *can't* do it, Dawlish, you must bring her back.'

Dawlish eased her fingers from his wrist and said gently:

'If the unknown Lia had a finger in Toby's death, she'll come back. People *are* like that. Even the Lucille's of this world.' He turned to the others. 'I'm going back to the Home Guard and Moreton. There might be a squeak or two out of the male prisoners. Look after the girls, Ted, or I'll have your blood.'

He was outside two minutes later.

There was no noise immediately overhead, although he could hear the sound of distant gunfire.

He slipped behind the wheel of Ted's Talbot, and started for

Staines. As he drove, the conversation he had had with Lucille passed through his mind.

Could he trust her?

He thought sardonically that 'trust' was a strange word to use in connection with Lucille, nevertheless he put his hopes in the possibility of dissension between her and the man she called Lia.

From dissension many things could spring.

He was nearing Chiswick when he first realized that he was being followed: it did not surprise him. He drove on, outwardly unconcernedly though prepared for immediate action.

The following car kept to within twenty yards of him, driven with side-lights only.

He did not try to go faster than the twenty-miles-an-hour black-out limit until he reached the wide stretch of the Great West Road. There was no traffic on the single-line carriageway immediately ahead, and he opened out to nearly forty miles an hour.

The following car kept pace.

Dawlish increased his speed to fifty before suddenly slowing down. The manoeuvre made it impossible for the driver behind him to judge what he was going to do. Dawlish's brakes squealed loudly, so did those of the car behind him. There was a moment when it seemed as if there would be a collision, but the following car drew up inches from the rear of the Talbot.

By then Dawlish was in the road.

He reached the other car before the driver could get his hands from the controls, and he flashed a torch into the other's face—to see the startled features of Mr. Forbes, Montgomery's second-in-command.

CHAPTER TWENTY-EIGHT

A GENTLEMAN IS OFFENDED

The man's hands dropped from the wheel.

Dawlish switched off his torch.

'Good evening,' he said, amiably. 'Not a very good night for driving, is it?'

Slowly Forbes relaxed.

It was clear, however, that he was not pleased. In fact his expression was one of a man who had been considerably offended, not to say frightened.

'What the devil do you think you're doing?' he demanded.

'It should be obvious,' said Dawlish curtly. 'Aren't I trusted, Forbes?'

'That's got nothing to do with it. I—who *are* you, anyway?'

'No, no, no,' implored Dawlish. 'If you were going to pretend to wide-eyed innocence, the time to start was much earlier.'

Forbes took a deep breath.

'I—oh, all right, Dawlish. I followed you. There's no purpose in beating about the bush. I—'

'I know,' said Dawlish. 'You didn't like my manner at the flat, you didn't like my treatment of a real live diplomat, and you had doubts about my honesty. Also, you were mortally offended by Montgomery, who should have trusted you more than he trusted me. Right?'

'Don't talk such nonsense,' snapped Forbes. 'I—'

An official voice interrupted him.

'Put that light out.'

Dawlish smiled in the darkness.

'Sorry, officer. I—'

It was his turn to be cut short.

'I should say you was sorry, and you'll be sorrier when you've paid the fine. Name and address, please.'

Dawlish slipped a hand to his pocket, while Forbes snapped testily:

'Officer, I am an official—'

'Don't care who you are. I don't have lights shone unnecessary on *my* beat, and I don't care who knows it.' The man turned a subdued flick of light on to the card which Dawlish held out to him. It was signed by Sir Archibald Morely and was, in fact, the permit from the police. The result was instantaneous.

'Sorry about that, sir. Anything I can do to help?'

'Not just now,' said Dawlish. 'Except that I want to leave a car on the road, here—it will be all right if I pull it up into the kerb, won't it?'

'Drive on to the grass,' said the constable.

'Do you mind?' Dawlish asked Forbes.

'Dawlish, what on earth are you up to?'

'You appear to be coming my way. Surely it will be easier to do so if we are both in the same car?' Dawlish said blandly.

With a smothered imprecation that served to show that he was even more offended than he had been a short while before, Forbes drove to the grass verge, and braked.

Dawlish opened the door for him.

'Good man,' he said. 'And thanks, constable.'

'Car'll be all right, sir,' said the constable. 'But oblige *me*, sir, an' be careful with that torch. No need to *abuse* your privileges, sir.'

Dawlish chuckled. 'Certainly not, constable.' He was urging Forbes towards the Talbot as he spoke. The constable held up an approaching car while they started off, and not until they had travelled a hundred yards or more did Dawlish say:

'Now tell me, Forbes. Why did you follow me?'

Forbes was still disgruntled, and Dawlish was prepared to believe at best that the man, caught in doing something at which he was not expert, was simmering with rage because he had failed to do it successfully.

But there was another, obvious, possibility.

There *was* somewhere at headquarters a leakage, and it could be through Forbes. Lucille's casual way of saying 'Lia learned' had been more informative than she had suspected.

He could have learned through Forbes.

It was a possibility, and Dawlish cursed the fact that it would be difficult to distinguish between a Forbes who was angry because he had been detected, and a Forbes who was afraid because he might be suspected.

'I know of no reason why I should not follow you,' Forbes said coldly.

'No?' asked Dawlish, and his voice went upwards a little. 'I don't think we quite understand each other, Forbes. I'm doing a job on my own and in my own way. I don't welcome interference. You might have upset a carefully made plan—'

'You should report all plans to me or Colonel Montgomery,' snapped Forbes. 'You take too much on yourself, Dawlish.'

'Such as?'

'You did not take Lucille Lefroy to Cannon Row.'

'No?' asked Dawlish.

'Don't try to be evasive,' Forbes said heatedly. 'You not only took her to your flat, but you allowed her to go free. No one followed her. I—'

'Go on,' said Dawlish.

'My engine stalled, or I would have done so,' said Forbes.

'I see,' said Dawlish, battening down a desire to let himself go as he had done to the officer of the Home Guard, except that for Forbes he had conceived a cold dislike which he had never felt for Moreton. 'Now we'll have some straight talking, Forbes. If you had done any such thing you would have wrecked the best chance of learning just what is happening. I don't ask you to try to see it my way, I'm just telling you. Now I'll tell you something else. When we get back to London, you'll report this to Montgomery, and undertake to make no more little sorties on your own. Is that clear?'

Forbes drew a deep breath.

'Dawlish—' the voice rose, and Dawlish saw that he was at a pitch of tension which he controlled only by a great effort, 'I shall continue to do what I consider my duty, without asking you, or—'

'Do you mean that?' demanded Dawlish abruptly.

'Of course I do. You'll have to act more carefully. I want a full explanation of where the woman went and why she was allowed to go.'

Dawlish did not answer.

There was silence in the car which dragged from seconds to minutes. They could hear the crump of bombs even above the noise of the engine, and the explosions seemed to get louder; Dawlish suspected that the raiders were dropping H.E.'s into the flames started—he thought—by their incendiaries.

Forbes broke the silence at last, his voice threatening to crack.

'You heard me, Dawlish.'

'Oh, yes,' said Dawlish. 'I heard you. I was wondering just how to reply.' He sounded as amiable as he had done when he had first spoken to Forbes by the car. 'Look here, I have to see some of the men who were taken prisoner when the woman was. They're likely to know as much as she does, you know. I let her go because I wanted to fly a kite which may or may not come off—but if I hadn't the prisoners up my sleeve I would have held the lady. Does that make sense to you?'

Forbes spoke quickly—so quickly that it appeared that he wanted to be conciliated.

'Why didn't you say that before?'

'You knew of the prisoners, Lucille didn't,' said Dawlish. 'I made the mistake of over-estimating your judgment.' That insult must have sunk in, but Forbes made no comment, and Dawlish drove on in silence. The crump of bombs had stopped, but a fire was still flaring away. They drew nearer, and Dawlish wondered which of the small factories in that direction had suffered.

He turned off the road towards Staines, as he had done earlier that day, when Lucille had been behind him. As he did so his muscles stiffened.

A fire engine clanged past him, and other cars going on the work of rescue followed, but he hardly noticed them. He saw the long, narrow building which was in flames nearest him. It was not a factory; he hated to think what it was, although from the time he had turned off the road he had been afraid.

The Home Guard building was on fire!

Two or three engines were already working on the flames, and the figures of firemen could be seen, silhouettes against the red glow. Houses beyond the 'Social Club' had been hit, and fires were also raging there. That in itself was grim; but to

Dawlish the thing that struck at his heart was the raging fire at the social club, the thought of the men who had done so fine a job, of Moreton . . .

And of the prisoners.

CHAPTER TWENTY-NINE

TIM JEREMY OVERHEARS

It was bad, but it could have been worse.

Moreton, it transpired, had been making a tour of inspection when the attack had first started.

The Home Guard Commander, smoke-grimed, with his clothes singed and in some places burned away, stood facing Dawlish in an A.R.P. station.

'The fire was started by bombs flung from a passing car, Dawlish. One landed on the roof, and it went up like matchwood—that's pretty well all it is,' he added grimly. 'A couple of bloody Huns started dropping their stuff then, but we had managed to get most of the men out before the bombs dropped. There was a direct hit on the club,' he added.

Forbes, apparently determined he should hear all there was to hear, stood by, smoking a Turkish cigarette: Dawlish disliked men who smoked Turkish cigarettes, and also disliked the smell of the smoke; in fact there were few things he could think of that were in Forbes's favour.

'We lost three of the prisoners,' Moreton said. 'The other four had to be rushed to hospital—they're badly hurt, I'm afraid.

Thank God only two of my men caught it—and they'll get better.'

'Dawlish!' Forbes's voice had the high-pitched note again. 'Do I understand that the prisoners are no longer available for questioning?'

'For a few days, yes,' said Moreton.

'And you actually—'

Dawlish turned furiously. It looked as if he would strike the man. 'Did you question them, Moreton?'

'They would say nothing.' Moreton was eyeing Forbes with obvious disfavour. 'But I learned one thing that was rather remarkable, Dawlish. The three that spoke at all were all Irish. The brogue was quite unmistakable.'

Dawlish smiled slowly.

'I half suspected that, and now it is confirmed. Oh, well, we can't do any more. Er—any hardship over the injured Home Guards, do you know?'

Moreton's lips were compressed for a moment.

'Clarke's wife will have a hard job, I'm afraid. What a filthy business it is!'

'Dependants will get allowances,' Forbes put in.

'After a month of argument,' snapped Moreton. He turned back to Dawlish. 'I shall help her all I can, but—'

'I know,' said Dawlish. 'A dozen calls on your purse, and you don't know which to answer first. However, we can't have Clarke's wife in trouble and Clarke worried while he's in hospital. My responsibility—I started it. I—'

'Now, Dawlish, you—'

'I'll put up a hundred pounds,' Dawlish said. 'You can distribute where you feel it will do most good—more to come when that's exhausted.' He took out his cheque-book. Moreton stared at him, as if too startled to realize what was happening, and Forbes cleared his throat impatiently. Dawlish handed over the cheque, and Moreton said slowly:

'This is a tremendous thing, Dawlish. I hardly know how to thank you.'

'You did that before this blasted bombing,' said Dawlish. 'Well, I'll get away.' He shook hands with Moreton, while Forbes turned towards the door. The man was outside and in the car first. Dawlish slipped into the driving-seat, and let out the clutch.

'Now perhaps you will realize the idiocy of letting the woman go,' snapped Forbes. 'It is always the same when regulations are ignored, I—'

'If you open your mouth on that subject again I'll ram your teeth down your unpleasant throat,' said Dawlish tersely.

'*What* did you say?'

'You heard,' said Dawlish. 'We're going to see Montgomery. Either you keep out of this business or I do. If they want it done by rule of thumb, God help them.'

They were silent then for the rest of the journey, although several times Forbes stirred. Dawlish had an idea that the man wanted to speak, but could not find a way of approach. Dawlish gradually forgot him, and even pushed the tragedy at the Home Guard unit to the back of his mind. He had known that sooner or later he would find himself dwelling on Tim Jeremy's fate more than he liked. He tried to tell himself that it was useless to speculate, but he longed for some means of finding out whether Tim was alive.

Tim Jeremy was not only alive, he was kicking.

He disliked the silent man who had tied his wrists too tightly after he had been taken from the wrecked car, surprised to find himself suffering from nothing more than a few cuts and bruises. He had also disliked the way in which the man had prodded him in the back when, after a journey lasting nearly two hours, he had been blind-folded and half-pulled from the car. Consequently, a little later in the evening, when the man brought him some cold water but not food, and struck him across the face when he protested, he kicked out; his shoe-cap caught the man on the knee, and the fellow gasped with pain as he staggered back.

Jeremy, his wrists still fastened behind him, was prepared for violence, when footsteps sounded in the passage outside.

The door opened, and Jeremy saw a tall, thin man, chinless, but impressive.

He eyed the captor coldly.

'What are you doing, O'Keefe?'

'O'Keefe,' said Tim Jeremy in the sepulchral voice which often startled those of his acquaintances who did not know him well, 'is suffering from a wallop on the knee-cap. He'll suffer some more if he doesn't learn to keep his hands to himself.'

O'Keefe did not speak. Julian Fesell—Lia to his friends— turned his eyes towards Jeremy, and stared down. Tim had a peculiar feeling, much—he imagined—as that of a rabbit hypnotized by a stoat.

'So,' said Fesell at last, 'you are one of those young men, are you?'

'It has been said,' admitted Timothy.

'I have never met one before,' said Fesell, and his eyes narrowed a little. 'I have, of course, heard of them. Dawlish is a particular example, I understand.'

'You might say the doyen of the breed,' agreed Timothy.

Fesell smiled; oddly enough, Tim found it attractive. It warmed the strange, chinless face, and made the man seem much more human. 'May I inquire your name?'

'Jeremy,' said Tim.

‘Oh, yes. A close personal friend of Mr. Dawlish's. You are in the Mid-Wessex Regiment, aren't you, stationed near York? I regret to have to say it, but I have read that you are not considered one of the intelligentsia amongst your friends.'

‘Don't regret that,' said Tim. ‘I'm proud of it.'

He was feeling considerably out of his depth.

He had an impression, moreover, that the newcomer was suffering from the same disadvantage; as if, in fact, the stoat having hypnotized the rabbit, was seized with a sudden fear that the rabbit might bite. There was a short period in which neither man spoke, and then Fesell drew a sharp, impatient breath.

‘Bring him to my study, O'Keefe, and do not use unnecessary force.'

The man assented sullenly, although Tim believed his sullenness was reserved for the prisoner who had kicked him; in fact Tim hoped that the knee was not only painful but that it would remain so indefinitely.

O'Keefe did not show a gun, but kept one hand in his pocket; as Tim went ahead of him, some half-a-minute after the tall newcomer had left the room.

They reached a flight of stairs.

It was narrow, and Tim had an idea that it had been recently built.

He reached a landing and a further flight of stairs.

As he stepped towards it, directed by O'Keefe, he felt the man's foot touch his right knee. It was a light touch, and could easily have been accidental, but it was enough to send Tim off his balance. He staggered, unable, with his hands tied behind him, to save himself.

He fell.

He did not land with any great force. Nevertheless, he lay there, winded, bruised, half-conscious.

He did not hear a door open, or men's voices.

'What is this?' Fesell demanded, and O'Keefe looked at him with surly triumph.

'The clumsy fool fell down the stairs.'

'Oh,' said Fesell. 'He fell down, did he? Help him up, at once.' The grey eyes turned towards a middle-aged man with long grey hair, which overlapped the sides of a pair of steel spectacles. 'You help also, Abel.'

Between them they lifted Jeremy, and carried him into the study where, earlier that day, Lucille Lefroy had taken her orders from Fesell. There was a couch in it, and here Tim was lowered. He was not wholly unconscious, but he feigned to be right out. He heard O'Keefe grunt.

'A can of water would bring him round.'

'It would also spoil my carpet,' said Fesell thinly. 'All right, O'Keefe, you may go.'

A door closed.

Tim was aware of two men near him; he could tell that more from their breathing than from any movement. He steeled himself to show no surprise at anything that happened, and thus was able to control his muscles when a hand rested for a moment against his cheek. Immediately after that Fesell spoke, in his curiously high voice.

'It would appear that there are limits which these hardy young men have to acknowledge. He is not, I think, badly hurt. Now tell me, Abel, why the disaster at St. John's Wood was necessary.'

Abel did not waste words.

Tim heard the story told from a different angle—of the discovery, after Bray and Pell had taken the prisoners downstairs, of the prisoners' escape. He, Abel, had pressed a switch which had sent the house up—as previously planned. It was, he said, the only thing he could do.

'And what happened to Bray?' asked Fesell.

'I have no idea.' Abel spoke in a curiously precise voice.

'And Pell?'

'I did not see either of them. They were in the cellar with Dawlish and the others. I assumed that Dawlish had taken them away. I do not know.'

'It is peculiar,' said Fesell, and he echoed the thoughts in Tim Jeremy's mind. He had felt sure that Fesell—whom he did not know by name—would know all there was to know of Bray. He was about to start the pretence of regained consciousness when there was a sharp ring of a bell. After a pause, and the lifting of something that might have been a telephone, Fesell said:

'Who is it . . . why, yes, of course, Lucille . . . yes, immediately. I am delighted to hear that you are back, I was afraid that Dawlish had . . . yes, I heard of the trouble, but never mind that now. Come downstairs at once, I shall be glad to talk to you.'

The telephone was replaced, and there was silence in the room. No word passed between the long-haired taxi-driver and Fesell until the door opened and Lucille entered. Tim changed his mind and lay still.

He detected the note of surprise in Fesell's voice.

'Why, Lucille, you look quite ill. Sit down, my dear.'

'I don't want to sit down,' said Lucille roughly, and even to Tim, who had to judge only from her voice, it was clear that she was labouring under the stress of considerable emotion. 'Where's Bray?' she demanded abruptly.

'He has not returned,' said Fesell.

'It's time he did.'

'We think perhaps that Dawlish has taken him.'

'I've just got away from Dawlish,' snapped Lucille, and Tim felt his heart drop. 'Bray isn't there—Dawlish doesn't know where he is. That double-crossing swine will try to get here sooner or later, and *I'll* handle him when he arrives.'

Fesell was very suave.

'My dear, you are obviously labouring under severe stress. What is it?'

Timothy did not know what she was going to say, but he did realize that whatever it was, it had a vital importance. It was as if he, too, felt the unseen and unsuspected presence of the dead Toby, and the utter silence in the room before she spoke told him that the other two men were equally conscious of a tension which her words might ease—and might make stronger.

But the words were a long time coming.

CHAPTER THIRTY

LOST LOYALTY

The temptation for Tim to open his eyes was so considerable that he actually did so for a split second. No one was looking towards him, however; the two men were staring at the woman, and she at them.

Slowly, and yet with an emphasis which seemed to make the words seem sharp, the woman answered.

'Bray killed Toby.'

To Tim Jeremy it would have made as much sense had she said that Mickey Mouse killed Donald Duck; but the tension in the room remained; indeed, the words increased it.

From the tall man the silky words came smoothly.

'Lucille, my dear! I am so sorry.'

Abel cleared his throat.

The woman looked from one man to the other, and then shrugged her shoulders.

'It's done, but what I want is to get my hands on Bray,' she said roughly.

Again Tim opened his eyes. He saw the tall man pouring a

drink with delicate movements—his hands were long, thin and white; like those of a doctor or a surgeon.

Lucille took the drink quickly. When she spoke again it was in a more normal voice.

'Who have you got here?'

'One of Dawlish's young friends,' said Fesell.

'So you managed to bring him, did you?' said Lucille.

She began to talk, explaining what had happened, and Timothy heard much that was interesting but nothing which was really informative, and certainly nothing that would help him in his present plight. She did not explain at great length how she had managed to get away from Dawlish, but said that she had been taken from one house to another, and had slipped away under cover of the darkness.

Tim thought: 'It doesn't ring true: people don't slip away from Pat.' He grew more sure than ever that she had been allowed to go, more hopeful that there would be developments in the next hour or so.

Fesell said:

'I was telephoned of your plight, my dear. I made all the efforts I could to have you freed, but Dawlish is a lucky as well as a resourceful young man. However, you have managed to get free. Now I wonder if the young friend could be awake—I have an idea,' he added gently, 'that he might have been awake for some time past. Is that so, Mr. Jeremy?'

Tim opened his eyes.

He smiled crookedly. His mouth was swollen but his eyes were alert.

He saw no object in lying.

'Yes,' he said amiably. 'I wondered whether you would guess. Pity you didn't give away something that mattered.'

'I am really not likely to be careless,' said Fesell. 'I should not allow you access to any vital information. However, I hope that you, in very different circumstances, will not feel the same, for I want to hear all that you can tell me. Abel, and O'Keefe, would not be averse to using methods of persuasion I assure you, but I somehow do not think you will make that necessary.'

Tim lifted his head.

'Quite right,' he said. 'I know so little that I can afford to tell you everything. But not at the moment.'

There was a slight tightening of Fesell's lips, nothing more.

'You are hardly in a position to make any conditions, are you?'

'Well, after all, it's my tongue,' said Jeremy in a reasoning tone, 'And its twin functions are to talk and taste. Now there may be times when talking comes first, but at the moment my view is that tasting is its paramount duty. Do I make myself clear?'

Fesell laughed, a low-pitched, clucking sound. There was no doubt that he was amused.

'Circumlocution *in extremis*,' he said. 'I have never heard anyone use so many words to say that they were hungry before. We can arrange a little food, however. I—'

He stopped abruptly.

One of the telephones on his desk shrilled out, and for a moment there was silence in the room. Then Fesell lifted the receiver. Timothy could not understand why the tension, which had eased somewhat, was suddenly back in the room. He did not know that it was because the telephone which rang was an outside one, and that at such an hour calls from outside were rare at White Lodge.

Fesell said softly: 'Yes, who is that?'

He paused for a moment, and then his eyes looked towards Lucille. Tim saw the expression, one of smouldering flame; it was not nice to think that a man could put so much into his eyes.

And then Tim wondered whether he had been imagining things, for the glow died away, and Fesell spoke as softly as before.

'I see, Martin, thank you very much. Good-bye.'

He replaced the receiver. Lucille finished her drink, and Fesell said in a faraway voice.

'I think perhaps Mr. Jeremy had best have his meal in his room—send for O'Keefe, Abel, and have him taken away. There are several things we shall want to discuss in private. I am inclined to believe Jeremy when he says that he does not know a great deal.'

Jeremy knew that the telephone message had brought bad news; he even wondered whether it could mean that the woman had been followed and that someone had discovered that Dawlish, Ted, and perhaps others were in the vicinity. He hardly knew whether to hope or to be afraid as he went upstairs, this time not assisted unduly by O'Keefe, who had been summoned by a bell.

He was taken to the small room where he had first seen O'Keefe and the chinless man. Within five minutes sandwiches and coffee were brought in on a tray. O'Keefe untied his wrists, but stood within a yard of him while he ate. O'Keefe's right hand remained in his pocket, and Tim strongly suspected he held a gun there.

He was nearly through the last sandwich when he heard footsteps outside the door. A hand tapped lightly.

'Unlock the door, O'Keefe.'

The man did not hesitate. He opened the door. Lucille stood there.

She eyed O'Keefe sharply.

'Go to your room,' she said, 'and wait there until Abel or I send for you.'

Again the Irishman obeyed without question. Tim was puzzled, and yet learned from it that the woman was as used to giving orders to the chinless man's servants as their employer himself. He saw her take the keys from O'Keefe, and she also took a small automatic from her handbag before the Irishman left the room. As his footsteps echoed along the passage the woman locked the door with an unnecessary rattle: even then Tim wondered why she made so much noise.

He looked into her eyes and then at the gun.

'What's this?' he inquired casually. 'Seduction under duress?'

For all the effect of his words he might not have spoken.

'You're Jeremy, aren't you?'

'I am.'

'Listen. I made a bargain with Dawlish, and I can't keep it.' Her words startled him. 'I'm going to try, through you. Are you badly hurt?'

'Only to look at.'

She thrust her automatic into his hand.

'I'm going out in two minutes. I daren't wait longer or they'll know where I am. I'll leave the door unlocked. Go down the first flight of stairs, and then, instead of going down the second, turn right. It looks like a blank wall. Press a small knob under the handrail, and a door will slide open. It will take you to a fire-escape. The village is about half a mile away—turn right from the drive. Do you understand?'

'Yes.' Jeremy was already on his feet, staring at her.

'Telephone Dawlish from the village. Tell him this is White Lodge, Winton, near Winchester. He'll know what to do. Tell him that everything he wants is here—the man I called Lia is Julian Fesell, well known in the village. Is that all clear?'

Tim said slowly: 'It's so clear that it sounds suspiciously like a "shot while attempting to escape" gambit,' he said. 'It could be a lost loyalty—'

'That's it,' she said, and there was bitterness in her tone. 'Lost loyalty.' The words made her laugh, although there was nothing to suggest that she was amused. 'Dawlish will know what it's about,' she said. 'Tell him Lia has realized that I know, and that he'll watch me too closely for me to get away. And tell him to remember his bargain, if he gets here in time.'

Tim felt like a man in a daze.

But he moved towards the door and opened it for her, and he heard her go along the passage after closing the door and making a noise with the keys. He waited until her footsteps had died away, and then he re-opened the door.

He was afraid, even then, that there was some trick. He kept the small automatic in his right hand and stepped swiftly along the passage. Tight-lipped and frowning a little he reached the landing at the foot of the first flight of stairs. He heard nothing. He stepped towards the blank wall, and ran his hand along the handrail.

He found the protuberance the woman had mentioned.

He half-expected to find men shooting at him when the door slid open, but nothing happened. He saw a faint translucent glow from the moon about the grounds which faced him.

He stepped through the door to an iron fire-escape.

It was then that he realized one thing she had forgotten— deliberately or not he did not know. He could not close the door from the outside, and the light from the passage showed clearly, attracting the attention of anyone in the grounds. And as he went down the fire-escape he heard a man's voice not far away.

'Where's that light coming from?'

Tim's heart jumped as he reached the ground, seeing two vague shapes not twenty yards away from him.

CHAPTER THIRTY-ONE

SHARP SHOOTING

There was a chance that he would get away unseen.

But the men were near enough to see the fire-escape, and they did not waste time looking into the passage. One said sharply:

'It ought to be closed.'

'There's someone!' snapped the other.

Tim knew then that he must shoot or be shot; there was no chance of dodging, for a long expanse of wall ran ahead of him, and until he reached the corner of the house the only way he could go except along the wall was into the arms of the watchers.

He fired once.

The sharp glow of the shot, and the loud report, seemed greater than they were because of the silence and the comparative darkness which preceded them. He saw one man stagger, and he ran a few yards, hoping that the second man would be too cautious to follow. He was not. The man came running, firing as he ran.

Tim did not run evenly.

He heard the loud report of the shot, and he knew that it would not be long now before others inside the house were attracted. There was a second shot, and a bullet whistled past his ear. He fired again, but he had no time to take aim, and his bullet went wide.

He heard doors opening, heard footsteps approaching, voices raised in inquiry. He reached the corner of the house unharmed, but saw two men approaching along the drive—and he had to get to the end of the drive. But he was in a better position for shooting, and he fired twice.

One man went down.

Tim had a slice of luck: in falling, the one man knocked against the other, and with a spurt that would have approached the sprint record, Tim reached the men and passed them.

But the ground seemed alive with men.

Oddly enough, no torches were shining. It was as if they did not want to attract more attention than they could help, and they knew that a few shots would be more easily explained away than a general flashing of torches. Tim pounded along the drive, feeling his blood pulsing through his ears, his heart racing. Normally he believed he could have gone much faster, but the accident and the things that had followed it had robbed him of the reserve of strength that he needed.

He heard bullets strike the gravel near him.

He did not hear the actual shots, and he knew that the men were using silencers on their automatics. He was afraid every moment that a bullet would bite into his back, but the iron drive-gates loomed up in front of him before he was touched.

Then he felt what seemed like a red-hot knife in his upper arm. He did not think that it had touched the bone; he did know that he could hardly use his left hand. He set his teeth and went on. He reached the drive, and turned right.

Ahead of him he saw a bend in the road.

He knew that if he could reach it he would be safe. There

were trees on either side of the road, and a hedge which dropped away abruptly to gorse-covered common-land.

He *must* reach it.

Footsteps pounded on the road behind him, and then above those sounds he heard that of a car engine. He believed that it was coming towards him, but he could not be sure.

Then he saw the glow of the side-lights.

He was now almost on a level with the gorseland, and he turned towards it. But as he did so the headlight was switched on. Dazzled by the beam, Tim was a vivid silhouette for the men who were behind him.

He flung himself downwards.

But quickly as he moved he was too late to avoid a second bullet, one that caught him in the thigh. It made him fall even more heavily than he had planned, and he could not get up once he was down. He stretched out, on his face, taking in great gulps of air, forgetful for the moment of the threat from behind him, oblivious to the fact that the car was drawing up with a great squealing of brakes, and that his pursuers were doubling back towards the drive of White Lodge, taking advantage of what shadows and darkness there was.

Had he known that, Tim might have laughed.

As it was he had to grit his teeth against the pain that flooded through him, pain in his shoulder, his thigh, his chest, in fact it seemed that every inch of his body was aching with the effort he had made.

Dawlish had not found it easy to get Tim out of his mind. But as he had neared Brake Street, and reached the *Dawnay Salon* he forced thoughts of him aside. He considered Forbes and Montgomery.

Why *had* Forbes followed him?

Had the man seen Lucille leave, and been unable to follow her solely because of the stalling of his engine, or had he, also, deliberately let her go?

If so—why?

That, thought Dawlish, was a question of paramount importance, but it was not going to be easy to answer. There were other things on his mind, however. Forbes's manner had been the reverse of helpful, and certainly nothing the man had said or done suggested that he was at one with his Chief in the desire for unorthodox methods to be put into action.

Was Forbes just a bad specimen of the *genus* Civil Servant? That could explain it.

Yet always there was the suspicion that there was some kind of a leakage in high places. It grew obvious that Forbes was the most likely suspect.

Forbes broke the long silence as Dawlish drew up.

'What are you going to report to Montgomery, Dawlish?'

Dawlish eyed him in the gloom.

'Just what happened,' he said. 'Worried?'

Forbes did not reply, and they went into the flat. Forbes had a key, but obviously their arrival had been seen, and the servant was waiting to take their hats and coats. A few seconds later they were in Montgomery's office, and the Colonel was standing by the fireplace, short, erect, frowning.

He said abruptly:

'Ah, Dawlish. Did the woman prove communicative?'

'She did not,' said Dawlish. 'I—'

'I really think that I should make a report first,' began Forbes, but he stopped abruptly when Dawlish gripped his arm. He did not try to interrupt when Dawlish began to speak, giving a resumé of what had happened from the moment he had left Brake Street with the prisoner. Forbes could have no complaint that only Dawlish's side of the story was presented: Montgomery had the whole of it, and Dawlish's manner suggested that he could do what he liked about it.

Montgomery heard him out without interruption.

Dawlish finished:

'And so here we are. Forbes is not pleased, but nor am I pleased with Forbes.'

Montgomery raised his hand.

'You won't be worried by personalities, Dawlish, and I hope you won't either, Forbes. It doesn't matter who succeeds in finding our men, nor how it is done. Obviously you acted in good faith, Dawlish. Whether it was wise to let the woman go can be decided only by the results.'

'Not quite,' said Dawlish. 'It's measured by the possibility of getting them. I don't think she would have told us anything at all if we'd kept her, and if she doesn't come back we've lost nothing. I think I would have let her go even had I known the other prisoners were to be released.' He was emphatic with the word 'released' and as he uttered it he thought of the bombing.

Montgomery pursed his lips.

'It's done, and talk isn't going to help us. She's told you a remarkable story, Dawlish. The I.R.A.—they *have* been very quiet in this country lately.'

'The thing of importance is the bullion,' said Dawlish.

'Yes, of course.' Montgomery's eyes were shadowed. 'There was such a matter for discussion, I know. It makes her story ring true. I'll have to get a report through as soon as possible—*if* we can rely on what she told you. That is the trouble. If she made the story up and I report it as facts discovered—well, you won't need telling it will be most unfortunate.'

Dawlish said gruffly.

'Kicks in the pants all round, yes.'

Forbes drew a deep breath.

'You mustn't make the report, Montgomery—at least, not until further evidence is forthcoming. It is the wildest guesswork at the moment—we shall be a laughing-stock if we make such a report and it is found to be false. More than a laughing-stock. We can hardly be expected to retain our positions—'

'That really worries you, doesn't it,' said Dawlish, and he eyed the man curiously. 'A funny world. Well, I'm going to sit back and wait for the time being, at all events. Unless there is anything else you want from me?'

'No-o.' Montgomery shook his head. 'Not at the moment, I think. It seems a little unlikely that we shall hear from the woman again, nevertheless, we must wait and see.'

Dawlish nodded, and went out. But before he had gone far he returned.

'Yes, Captain Dawlish?'

'About Bray,' said Dawlish. 'Who reported that he had escaped?'

'The rescue squad which reached the house,' said Montgomery.

'Who took the report?'

'Why, Forbes I believe—isn't that so, Forbes?'

The man nodded. Dawlish shrugged, and withdrew again. He was in thoughtful mood as he climbed into his car.

Entering Jermyn Street his headlamps picked up the figure of a man, tall and gangling, turning into the doorway of No. 55, the old and burned flat. Dawlish fancied there was something familiar about the man. He hopped out of the car, and followed the other in the dimly lit hall. The man was peering at the cards which were on a board and gave the names of the several tenants.

He turned sharply; Dawlish's fancy had not been a wrong one, for it was Jo Whipple, of King's Cross.

'Oh—it's you, sir.' Whipple seemed neither pleased nor sorry. 'Got that address you wanted, sir. Cove what started the trolly, remember. Got 'is name too. Soon as I did, I ses, I'm going to see that Capting, I ses to meself, pay 'im aht better than I can, I ses.'

'Good chap,' said Dawlish, his heart was beating fast. 'What is the name, Jo?'

'O'Keefe, sir, that's the monniker. O'Keefe. Got it writ down.' From his overcoat pocket he drew out a crumpled piece of paper, on which were the words:

'J. O'Keefe, c/o White Lodge,
Winton, Nr. Winchester, Hants.'

Dawlish put the paper carefully in his pocket, and then took out his wallet.

'How on earth did you do it?' he demanded.

Jo Whipple eyed the wallet with a speculative expression.

'Out with it,' said Dawlish, extracting five one-pound notes.

'Blimey!' said Whipple. 'Ta.' He stowed the notes away with careful method. His moustache twitched. 'It wasn't on his case, sir. I see him, an' I ses to meself, that's 'im, I ses, so when he's buying a paper I picks up his case—worried 'im proper. Lorst, I ses it was. Told him I'd fahnd it unattended, and wouldn't give 'im it back until he'd give me his name and address. Writ it down himself for me, sir—that's the paper you've got.'

'Jo,' said Dawlish, 'you're a genius. I'll come along to King's Cross one day, and we'll have a drink together.'

'Right, sir.' Jo gave a half salute, buttoned his coat more securely over the five pounds and ambled out.

Dawlish made his way to Scotland Yard.

Trivett had been busy all day on the assassination case, but his manner did not suggest that he had gained any very cogent results. He looked, in fact, a weary man as he nodded to Dawlish.

'I suppose you've got nowhere,' he said gloomily. 'And I'm stuck. It's the biggest swine of a business I've come across.' His eyes narrowed. 'You look as if you've been in the wars.'

Dawlish smiled.

'Yes, I've had some fun and games, but that's by the way. I want to get in touch with the rescue squad which worked at the St. John's Wood house. Can you do it for me?'

In five minutes Trivett had contacted by telephone the station that had controlled the rescue and demolition activities at the house in St. John's Wood. In six, Dawlish was holding the receiver.

Trivett saw the big man's face harden, heard a sudden sharpening of his voice.

'Are you quite sure of this?'

'Oh, yea. There's not the faintest doubt about it.'

'Can I see the bodies?' Dawlish asked.

'Yes, that will be O.K. You should have a permit, of course . . .'

Dawlish turned to Trivett as he replaced the receiver. He said quietly:

'Bill, I think the band is going to start playing at last.'

'And the tune?' asked Trivett sourly.

'This,' said Dawlish, and he spoke for several minutes, keeping his voice low. Trivett at first protested, and then pulled a telephone towards him. He gave certain instructions, and then called for Detective Sergeant Munk.

'Detail five men for immediate action,' he said briefly. 'They're to be waiting here for word by telephone. When they're ready, you go to Brake Street—outside the *Dawnay Salon*—and wait there.'

'What, now?' demanded Munk, who had worked with the Inspector long enough for him to occasionally let it be seen that he considered himself put upon.

'Don't talk back,' said Trivett ill-temperedly.

Dawlish drove him at speed to the St. John's Wood house, where the demolition and rescue squads had their headquarters. A grey-haired man in flannels, whose eyes were red-rimmed and heavy with lack of sleep, greeted them. He nodded to Trivett, whom he knew.

'You were lucky,' he said. 'We were going to bury them early in the morning.'

'They were definitely found in that house?' Dawlish said.

The man looked slightly aggrieved.

'I hope you're not suggesting our records are wrong, sir. I superintended the work myself.'

'No slight intended,' said Dawlish. 'I'd been told that no one was brought out.'

'Somone used their imagination,' said the man, and a few moments later he unlocked the door of a room which was being used temporarily as a morgue. The light was poor, and showed little—but it showed enough.

The faces of Sebastian Bray and Chauffeur Pell were clearly recognizable. Dawlish would have sworn to the identification anywhere. Trivett drew a sharp breath.

'It's Bray, all right.'

Dawlish said oddly: 'Yes, it's Bray. Let's get to a telephone again, Bill.'

As Dawlish started the car off on the way to Brake Street, Trivett said quietly:

'Which one is it, Pat? Montgomery or Forbes?'

CHAPTER THIRTY-TWO

MONTGOMERY OR FORBES?

Dawlish did not answer for some seconds. Then:

'I don't know, but I could make a guess. You told Munk to get the place surrounded, didn't you?'

'Yes.'

'And you arranged with the exchange to see what calls had been sent out from Brake Street in the past hour?'

'You heard me do it,' said Trivett with a touch of irritation.

'So I did,' said Dawlish. 'It's like seeing a mermaid, Bill, one doesn't believe it. Montgomery or Forbes?' He relapsed into silence.

From a telephone kiosk near *Dawnay's Salon*, and with Detective Sergeant Munk in sight, Trivett called the Yard. Inquiries had been going apace, and there were results. A priority call had been put through from the Brake Street flat three-quarters of an hour earlier. A man had spoken. The call had been to Winton, Hampshire, 119. No record had been made of the conversation.

Trivett told Dawlish, who nodded bleakly.

'It's what I expected. As soon as I told the story, someone

'phoned to the mysterious Lia from here, and told him of the bargain I struck with Lucille. Even if she tried to get away Lia would stop her. Oh, well, let's get in.'

As he spoke a police car drew up, and five men climbed out. Three men were detailed to the rear of the premises, two others and Munk stayed in the street. Dawlish rang the bell at the front door, and was admitted by the colourless-looking servant.

'Yes, sir,' said the man in answer to Dawlish's inquiry, 'they are both upstairs.'

As Trivett and Dawlish reached the door of the office, they heard the sound of voices. They were raised voices and angry ones, Montgomery's predominating.

'I tell you, Forbes, that Dawlish will act as he thinks best. I won't have this continual complaining. Try to realize that your job is to get results, not to tie pieces of red tape where you think they'll look pretty.'

Dawlish's eyes took on a momentary gleam of humour.

Forbes' reply was high-pitched and aggrieved.

'That's all very well, but I don't trust the man. I've never heard such nonsense as letting the woman go. It could easily have been pre-arranged. We've known all along that they were after a bullion shipment if it were made—Dawlish could use a share of that.'

Trivett would have gone on; Dawlish rested a hand on his arm to stop him.

Montgomery's voice fell to a lower, angry note.

'Forbes, if you persist in this endeavour to malign Dawlish I shall be compelled to take disciplinary measures. Your actions have been the reverse of commendable for some time. I told you to check on the details of the report from the St. John's Wood house—did you?'

'I had other instructions—'

'You dallied too long in obeying the first,' snapped Montgomery. 'I also told you to check the report that Bray and his chauffeur had been seen at the airfield. Did you?'

'You told me to do something else—I've spent all day at the Ministry of Information, and you know it.'

'I assumed that you would have time to do what I asked without spending so much attention on your personal affairs,' said Montgomery acidly. 'I think it would be wise if you considered yourself temporarily suspended, Forbes.'

And then Dawlish opened the door.

He did so without knocking, and both men looked round, startled. Dawlish said drily:

'A good idea, Colonel. Forbes had better be under close arrest, too.'

Forbes swung round, his face drained of colour. Dawlish put out a hand and gripped his arm. For ten seconds Forbes swore at him viciously. It was Montgomery who stopped the outburst.

'That's quite enough, Forbes. Dawlish, what do you mean by "close arrest"?'

Dawlish shrugged.

'Forbes will tell you more than I can. But if you're looking for an explanation of the fact that he did not confirm Bray's escape, you have it in the fact that Bray was killed, with his chauffeur. Bray, therefore, was never at the airfield. It was just as well that Forbes had personal matters to attend to, and other instructions which he could use as an excuse for not confirming these items. Isn't that so, Forbes?'

Forbes drew a deep breath.

'It—it's all a lot of nonsense! I—'

'We haven't time to go into that,' said Dawlish roughly. 'We've enough evidence to prove our case, and while we get busy we'll have Forbes looked after.' He motioned to the telephone, and Trivett picked it up, contacted the Yard and asked:

'Have you found the address of Winton 119 yet?'

'Yes, sir,' said the operator. 'It is called White Lodge, a building on the southern side of the village. As instructed, I have told the local police to stand by, and advised Home Guard concentrations in the neighbourhood.'

Trivett rang off as Dawlish urged Forbes through the open door. Forbes went silently, like a man who could not fight against forces which had overwhelmed him.

Outside, Trivett said to Munk:

'Keep the prisoner closely confined, Munk—in my office will be best. I'll telephone further instructions.'

Dawlish was already at the wheel of the Talbot, Trivett beside him. Montgomery climbed in at the back. Conversation was not attempted by any of the three.

Dawlish drove swiftly through London, anxious only to get to Winton. He had thought fleetingly of calling for Ted, but decided that worthy was doing a better job looking after Felicity and Julia.

It was cold in the car, and grew colder once they were on the open road and speeding first to Basingstoke, and then to Winchester. Trivett, who had once worked in a country area, knew Winton well enough to be able to guide Dawlish once they had passed through the cathedral town.

'Steady here, Pat. The house is on the right, I think.' His voice sharpened. 'What's happening in front there?'

The headlamp showed up very clearly the figure of a man, staggering, falling. From way off came the sound of shooting.

Dawlish put on the brake sharply.

'That's Tim,' he said. 'I—'

He stopped, eased off the brakes, and started forward again. Trivett knew that was the right thing to do, and yet realized how much Dawlish would want to see whether Tim Jeremy was badly hurt. Montgomery sat upright in his seat, peering out of the side window.

Dawlish swung the car into the drive.

It was not a long one, and the front of White Lodge, now camouflaged in shades of green and grey, showed up clearly in the headlamp. So did two or three men, dodging under cover of shrubs and trees on either side.

Montgomery said sharply:

'We are going to be heavily outnumbered—look, Trivett— look at those men there!'

Trivett looked—and Montgomery pulled his right hand from his pocket. In it was an automatic, and the gun was poked sharply into Trivett's ribs. Montgomery's voice came hard and clear.

'Dawlish, pull up in front of the house and don't move— understand, don't move.'

Gently Dawlish answered him.

'That's fine, Colonel. I wondered how long you would hold your hand. You framed Forbes nicely, didn't you? But I didn't think much of Forbes as the bright man of your party.'

Dawlish jammed on the foot and hand brakes. The car pulled up so sharply that Montgomery was jolted forward. Trivett had been waiting for just such a moment, and he wrenched the gun from Montgomery's hand. Montgomery gave a harsh laugh.

'You damned fool, the place is crowded with men, you'll never get away with it!'

Even as he spoke, shooting started. The bullets smacking against the side of the car.

CHAPTER THIRTY-THREE

SAYS DAWLISH

The shooting grew into a positive fusillade, but it did not last for long. Dawlish said casually:

'A little surprise for you Colonel. We 'phoned instructions for armed police and Winchester Home Guard units to be on the premises. Look after him, Bill.'

Trivett lost no time.

He took a pair of handcuffs from his pocket, and fastened Montgomery to a handle of the car. It was not comfortable, but it was likely to be effective. Dawlish was already approaching the front door, and as he reached it two small lorries came along the drive. Home Guard in uniform and with rifles jumped down, and Dawlish, for the second time, knew something of the efficiency and readiness of that volunteer army.

It seemed an anti-climax to press the bell.

But he did so, while an officer pushed forward.

'There's a very extensive air-raid shelter here, sir—they might use that.'

'And probably will,' said Dawlish. 'There'll be exits in the grounds, too—how many men are watching?'

In the faint light from the car he saw the man smile.

'Two hundred, sir.'

'Oh, good work! Well, it doesn't look as if we're going to get in without trouble. Have the side window smashed, will you.' He stood back while men used the butts of their rifles, then with a hand through the broken window, he found the catch and bolts of the door. Pushing them back he flung the door wide. The passage beyond was empty and silent. He half-expected opposition from the stairs or the rooms on either side. There was none. He shone the powerful beam of his torch about.

And then suddenly he heard footsteps, and as he looked ahead he saw a man coming into sight from the rear of the house—a man with long, grey hair and steel-rimmed spectacles. He was carrying an automatic, but that was less important than the fact that he was limping badly. When he saw Dawlish he raised his gun—but Dawlish was near enough to twist it from the man's hand.

Abel gasped.

Dawlish hit him. The man thudded to the floor, and then there was a strange silence inside and outside the house; the shooting had stopped.

Trivett was behind Dawlish.

'The place seems empty,' he said.

'Upstairs it probably is,' said Dawlish. 'They can't have too many men, and they've lost a lot today. They've had a chase in the grounds after Tim, so most of them would be outside. And our cabby, I think, was coming *via* the back door to tell Lia and the others that all is lost. This, I think, should lead us somewhere,' he said grimly, pointing to a door beneath the stairs. The handle turned, and the door opened, but there was no sound from below.

Dawlish went down, with Trivett a step behind him.

As they neared the passage at the foot of the stairs they heard a faint murmur of voices. They were coming from behind a heavily studded oak door. There was an iron handle, and Dawlish turned it very slowly.

For the first time in his life he heard the thin voice of Julian Fesell.

'You were very foolish, my dear,' it said. 'I realized, of course, that your devotion to your brother was considerable, but I did not think it was as firmly established as this. I feared you might be persuaded to talk if you went back to Dawlish—you see, my dear, I heard all about your remarkable bargain. I have an informant who keeps me well posted. But I did not think you would be foolish enough to free Jeremy.'

There was no answer.

Dawlish pushed the door an inch or two further open. He could see the woman standing opposite Fesell, who was sitting at his desk. A man with his back towards Dawlish was holding his right hand in his pocket: Dawlish did not know then that his name was O'Keefe.

'However, no great harm has been done,' went on Fesell. 'You should really understand by now that I have everything very well under control. My private interests come first, of course, but my devotion to the cause of the I.R.A. had forged a loyalty in my helpers which is far greater than yours. They are now patrolling the grounds, and I expect Abel to return with news of Jeremy's capture within a few minutes. But'— Fesell leaned forward—'if he does *not* report within ten minutes I shall know that Jeremy has escaped, and that this house will no longer be serviceable. You see this little button here?'

He touched a green button built into the desk. The woman's eyes turned towards it, and Fesell went on softly:

'It will destroy the house just as St. John's Wood was destroyed. There is another switch, in the drive gates. I shall press the one on those gates, on my way to safety, but you will remain here. Do you understand, Lucille?'

She still said nothing.

Dawlish stepped forward, very softly, Trivett followed him. In both men's mind was the thought of the little green button, and what it could mean. Both men breathed lightly, desperately afraid of making the slightest noise. They reached the inner door, which was nearly a foot open, and Dawlish put his hand on the handle. As he moved the door there was a sharp buzz inside the room.

Swiftly he pulled it wider, a sudden fear within him. He saw Lia turn sharply in his chair, and he saw O'Keefe take his right hand from his pocket. There was a gun in the Irishman's hand.

O'Keefe used it.

Dawlish felt the wind of the bullet pass his face, and at the same time saw Lia move his right hand towards the green button. It all happened very swiftly, even before he could fire. He touched the trigger of his automatic as a second bullet from O'Keefe splintered the glass of a door-panel. He saw a splotch of red spring into Lia's hand, but the man had touched the green button; *and he pressed, keeping his finger there.*

A fantasia of thought and fear and memory went through Dawlish's mind in that moment: of the journey south, the meeting with Tim and Ted, the oddness of Montgomery's manner from the start of the affair. Of Julie Dawnay and her story of her father, of the lie Montgomery told about Bray— as clever a move as there could be, for Dawlish could have wasted a lot of time looking for a dead man. Of the cleverness of Montgomery's effort to incriminate Forbes and clear himself of possible suspicion—even to giving Forbes orders that countermanded others.

All the time these thoughts flashed through Dawlish's mind, the patch of red was growing larger on Julian Fesell's hand, but the man's finger remained on the press-button. Dawlish was unaware of time, only of rushing thoughts.

He saw Lucille; not in front of him and staring at Lia, but bending over the bonnet of the old Austin, lovely and appealing. She had carried out her bargain, or had done her best to: even to freeing Tim. He wondered if Tim was all right. And Felicity, darling Felicity.

His lips twisted. The explosion was a long time coming, but he did not doubt that it would come. And time was of no account now. Lia, odd, chinless man, would as lief die here as on the gallows.

Was there anyone else who could take control of the records?

Would the police manage to get them?

Dawlish's mind suddenly became aware of time again. It might have been a minute since the switch had been pressed, or ten seconds, or five minutes, but by then the explosion should have started. He was beginning to grasp the fact that the detonation was a failure, when Lucille Lefroy spoke. She did so in a low-pitched voice that held the touch of mockery which he knew so well.

'Quite wrong, Lia. I cut the wire before you brought me down here. It won't blow up in a thousand years.'

It did not blow up.

To Dawlish—and to Trivett—it was like a nightmare with a dream-ending. They began to move as she spoke, and Dawlish shot O'Keefe's gun from his hand. Fesell sat motionless, his blood-stained hand on the green press-button. Lucille turned away from him, and approached Dawlish.

'Well?' she said.

'I think yes,' said Dawlish, without saying what he meant to Trivett.

After that, things happened with surprising speed. Fesell made no attempt to fight. O'Keefe was helpless. There were no others in the house but Abel, who remained unconscious until he awakened in a Winchester police-cell. The many so-called guests of White Lodge had been patrolling the grounds on Fesell's orders; the Winchester police and Home Guard had had no difficulty with them.

Tim Jeremy was found, and within an hour in hospital: by dawn the report was satisfactory, and by breakfast time Julia Dawnay was with him.

Lucille . . .

Lucille had gone; she had slipped out of the car when he had stopped it on the road near London. He had started from White Lodge with her—Trivett had remained behind. Trivett, he imagined, would not ask a lot of questions as to how she had escaped. He was, in any case, too busy going through the I.R.A. and other private records at the house. But before that developed Trivett telephoned Dawlish, who had reached the Jermyn Street flat just after dawn.

'You'll want to know this, Pat. Montgomery's dossier is here— he has been in the Army a long time, but was nearly cashiered in the Sinn Fein days for sympathy with the I.R.A. He managed to bluff his way out of it. He did some Secret Service work in Ireland in those days, that's how he managed to get his present position—an expert on the Irish problem, or so it was believed. Correct credentials of course—'

'All good and proper,' said Dawlish. 'Oh, well, there aren't many of the breed, thank God. Anything else?'

'I can tell you that it was Fesell who arranged the misdirection of shipments in Ireland—through the I.R.A., of course. And something else I doubt if you've realized—'

'My guess first,' said Dawlish. 'The misdirection of deliveries of various goods had nothing at all to do with beating Britain's delivery promises, that was incidental. It was careful preparation so that when the bullion arrived in Ireland that also could be misdirected. Right?'

Trivett chuckled.

'Right. You're an amazing fellow, Pat. When did you first guess that?'

'Amazing be blowed,' said Patrick Dawlish. 'Mere, dogged commonsense. As far as this country was concerned deliveries were through in fair time—what the Irish did after taking delivery wasn't our pigeon. So it looked like preparation for something larger. The moment I heard "bullion" I knew what. All right?'

'You'll do,' said Trivett, and he rang down.

Felicity was at Dawlish's elbow. Ted had gone out—to sleep, he said, and to try to forgive Dawlish for leaving him out of the final showdown. Felicity's green-grey eyes, a little tired, were smiling.

'So it's all over,' she said thankfully.

'Well, yes, my darling—this little escapade is, certainly.'

'You mean, you *can't* mean . . .'

'No, no, of course not.' There was reassurance in his quick denial; but regret too. 'Oh, Lord, that reminds me, that poor devil Forbes is still in jail. I'd better telephone our Sergeant Munk.'

'Wasn't Forbes in it?'

'Good heavens no, he hadn't the brain.'

Dawlish lifted the telephone, his smile deepening as he watched Felicity.

Even as he talked to Munk he was thinking of her. Nor did he want to do anything else.

ABOUT THE AUTHOR

John Creasey, born in 1908, was a paramount English crime and science fiction writer who used myriad pseudonyms for more than six hundred novels. He founded the UK Crime Writers' Association in 1953. In 1962, his book *Gideon's Fire* received the Edgar Award for Best Novel from the Mystery Writers of America. Many of the characters featured in Creasey's titles became popular, including George Gideon of Scotland Yard, who was the basis for a subsequent television series and film. Creasey died in Salisbury, UK, in 1973.

THE PATRICK DAWLISH MYSTERIES

FROM OPEN ROAD MEDIA

EARLY BIRD BOOKS

FRESH DEALS, DELIVERED DAILY

Love to read?
Love great sales?

Get fantastic deals on bestselling ebooks delivered to your inbox every day!

Sign up today at
earlybirdbooks.com/book

9 781504 098663